D0796512

Jean-Philippe Toussaint

Naked

A NOVEL

Translated by
Edward Gauvin

DALKEY ARCHIVE PRESS

Originally published in French as *Nue* by Les Éditions de Minuit in 2013.

© Les Éditions de Minuit, 2013
Translation copyright © 2016 by Edward Gauvin

First Dalkey Archive edition, 2016

Library of Congress Cataloging-in-Publication Data

Names: Toussaint, Jean-Philippe, author. | Gauvin, Edward, translator.
Title: Naked / Jean-Philippe Toussaint ; translated by Edward Gauvin.
Other titles: Nue. English
Description: First Dalkey Archive edition. | Victoria, TX : Dalkey Archive
   Press, 2016. | "Originally published in French by Les Editions de Minuit
   in 2013" -- Verso title page.
Identifiers: LCCN 2016010763 | ISBN 9781628971408 (pbk. : alk. paper)
Subjects: LCSH: Women fashion designers--Fiction. | Man-woman
   relationships--Fiction. | GSAFD: Love stories.
Classification: LCC PQ2680.O86 N8413 2016 | DDC 843/.914--dc23
LC record available at https://lccn.loc.gov/2016010763

Partially funded by a grant by the Illinois Arts Council, a state agency.

This translation was published with the support of Ministère de la Fédération Wallonie-Bruxelles

www.dalkeyarchive.com

Victoria, TX / McLean, IL / Dublin

Dalkey Archive Press publications are, in part, made possible through the support of
the University of Houston-Victoria and its programs in creative writing, publishing,
and translation.

Printed on permanent/durable acid-free paper

"To write of her that which has never been written of any other woman." ~ Dante

Fall-Winter

Apart from the spectacular aspect of certain dresses Marie had created in the past—the dress of sorbet, the dress of rosemary and thorny broom, the dress of gorgonian coral adorned with necklaces of sea urchin and earrings of Venus-ear shell—Marie sometimes ventured beyond fashion into speculative territories akin to the most radical experiments of contemporary art. Developing a theoretical reflection on the very idea of haute couture, she had returned to the original meaning of the word *couture* as the sewing of cloth using different techniques, stitching, tacking, hooking, binding, which allow fabrics to be combined on models' bodies, twinned to the skin, and joined together, to present this year in Tokyo a haute-couture dress without a single stitch. With her dress made of honey, Marie invented a dress without straps or ties that clung all by itself to the model's body, a levitating dress, light, fluid, liquefying, slowly molten and syrupy, weightless in space yet wedded to the model's body, since the model's body was the dress itself.

The dress of honey had been shown for the first time at the Spiral building in Tokyo. It was the culmination of Marie's latest fall-winter collection. At the end of the show, the final model emerged from the wings wearing that dress of light and amber, as if her body had been dipped head-to-toe in a humongous jar of honey before her entrance. Naked and honeyed, flowing, she made her way down the catwalk, swaying her hips in time to the beat of the music, high-heeled, smiling, trailed by a swarm of bees that formed a thrumming procession midair, the honey their lodestone, an elongated, abstract cloud of droning insects that accompanied her parade and turned with her at catwalk's end in a yawing whirl like an outflung, disheveled scarf, sinuous and alive, writhing with the hymenoptera that followed in her wake when she made her exit.

That, at least, was the theory. In practice, the difficulties had multiplied, and showing the dress of honey at Spiral had required months of work and setting up a little cell devoted exclusively to the project. Right from the start, there was a choice to be made between using real insects or resorting to a system of artificial, remote-controlled bees, drawing on the latest bio-robotic research, which made it possible to imagine tiny flying robots rigged with ventral sensors.

After looking into the matter, and much exchange of email between Tokyo and Paris, brightened by adorable attachments containing complex diagrams for miniature winged prototypes with the sibylline allure of Da Vinci's flying machines, it appeared to be technologically feasible to make a swarm of bees fly down a fashion catwalk. The main point in favor that Marie's colleagues brought to light was that bee colonies are obedient and blindly follow their queen everywhere (should a queen manage to escape the hive, the entire colony follows her into the wild, so certain beekeepers don't think twice about clipping their queens' wings to prevent such an exodus). On an early preparatory trip to Japan, Marie's assistant had arranged for her to see a Corsican beekeeper who lived in Tokyo, and Marie had found herself in a restaurant with a panoramic view of Shinjuku, at lunch with a certain Monsieur Tristani, or Cristiani (whose first name was none other than Toussaint), a short, friendly, easygoing fellow dressed in beige-and-burgundy herringbone tweed. Monsieur Tristani had a cast on one wrist and his arm in a sling, he wore thick yellow glasses with tinted lenses that hid a keen, wily, suspicious gaze.

Monsieur Tristani had ordered an aperitif in the panoramic restaurant's deserted main dining room, and he must have been expecting a romantic luncheon with a young woman

interested in how honey is made, but it wasn't Marie's
habit to banter during a working lunch. No sooner had the
maître d' taken their orders than she explained, in a firm
voice, the broad outlines of her project. Monsieur Tristani,
whose ardor had soon been snuffed, listened solemnly, nodding, wrist in a cast, now and again ineptly hacking at a
filet of sole with his good hand, and then, setting down
his fish knife, he picked up his fork and gulped down a
mouthful with a pained, even preoccupied look, for if he'd
understood correctly, the idea was to cover a supermodel in
honey. *Piombu!* Monsieur Tristani didn't have much in the
way of answers to Marie's many queries, content to dodge
her questions with a vague wave of his hand and a fatalis-
tic expression, and taking up his fish knife once more, he
began to pry apart his filet of sole lengthwise, sometimes
sneaking a longing glance at the administrative buildings
of Shinjuku stretching into the fog beyond the wall of glass.
He remained resolutely confused, supplying evasive or irrel-
evant answers to the precise technical questions Marie had
readied for him (her planner, beside her on the tablecloth,
open to a list of questions she ticked off one by one), to
which she received not a single useful reply. You'd think
Toussaint knew nothing about bees (or that beekeeping was
just his cover).

Their collaboration had ended there, in the hotel lobby after lunch they'd gone their separate ways and, before taking his leave, he'd offered her a jar of honey (which had given Marie the idea for the subtitle to her show: "Autumn Maquis'). In the end, Marie had worked with a more bohemian bee-keeper, a German who had lived in the Cévennes and then on the island of Hokkaido, ever so slightly gay and crazy in love with her, she claimed (or just the opposite, said I: a crazy queen who had a slight crush on her), who never con-tradicted a soul and was ready to do whatever she wanted with his bees, provided the right releases and disclaimers were signed for the Japanese health authorities, and she forked over a pile of dough. That man would've been perfect had he not taken on the services of another German from the Cévennes who now also lived on Hokkaido (the kind of visionary idealist that honey draws like flies these days), who prided himself on training the queen bee for the catwalk, and who had given a staggering demonstration thereof in the Tokyo office of the Let's Go Daddy-O fashion house, in front of Marie's entire staff of Japanese colleagues, artists, and designers all in black with slim titanium steel-frame glasses, man-bag straps crisscrossing their chests, solemn and skeptical, gathered in a semicircle before an empty tres-tle table where, without a bee in sight, the fellow had treated them to a pathetic flea-circus act, that old chestnut where the ringmaster, upon losing his performers and calling out to them by name, finds them again, then puts them through acrobatics and death-defying triple somersaults (everyone had emerged from that meeting filled with consternation— and Marie had sent the guy packing).

Readying the dress of honey had also brought up several thorny issues involving laws, insurance, and contracts. When, after a lengthy casting session held at the Tokyo office of the fashion house Let's Go Daddy-O, the model for the honey dress was chosen at last, a young Russian girl barely seventeen years old, Marie's lawyers labored for more than a month to finalize the definitive contract with the Rezo Agency in Shibuya, a contract of more than fifteen pages that contained scores of codicils and unusual clauses due to the singular nature of the service provided. The model was asked to undergo several medical examinations, made to see a dermatologist and an allergist, and tests were scheduled at a private clinic to confirm that her skin could withstand, without risk of eczema or irritation, heavy contact with honey all over her body. There were no bees at the first rehearsals (the first hive, coming from Hakodate by truck, wouldn't arrive until the night before the show). Spiral had been entirely refitted, its shops and café closed to the public, and the catwalk built as an extension of the famous spiral ramp that descended from the mezzanine along white marble walls. All the building's broad windows had been obscured by giant black velour drapes. The dress rehearsal took place under the same conditions as the actual show, among amber followspots, electricians perched on ladders to adjust the positioning of the lights. The stage was covered with thick, silvery, protective tarps, and the supermodel, in white, untied sneakers and a pale-blue, yellow-flowered bikini, an iPod at her waist that a muddle of tangled wires connected to her ears, made a series of starts, timed by assistants laden with tech equipment. Laptops were strewn about backstage, forgotten here and there on the floor. Marie's full staff of Japanese colleagues had now taken up quarters at Spiral. They'd annexed the rows of lacquered black chairs reserved for the audience at the foot of the catwalk and were watching the model complete a series of full test runs starting from the wings, neither in honey nor followed by bees, coming down the catwalk in her untied sneakers and nonchalant stride, sulky of pout and ethereal of step, while the sound technicians, emerging from a jumble of silver flight cases, adjusted the levels from behind their consoles, occasionally interrupting the music only to let it resume in abrupt, booming fits and starts.

The day of the show, a few minutes before the dress of honey

made its entrance, a hive-like ferment reigned backstage.
The model, standing on a small step stool set on a transparent tarp, was waiting, naked, skin smooth and sex shaven,
in nothing now but a flesh-toned G-string barely an inch
wide masking her mons, and several makeup artists, standing beside her, were working on the parts of her body that
would remain uncovered during the show, dusting her face
and hands with rice powder, which they applied with powder puffs to bring out her skin against the amber of the
honey dress she wasn't yet wearing. Farther back, by shelves
full of alembics, round-bottom flasks, decanters, and graph-
ite crucibles, a swarm of androgynous Japanese assistants
bustled like lab techs about the stainless-steel vat that held
the honey, sliding test tubes into the sticky substance to
gather samples whose color and viscosity they studied with
magnifying glasses, sticking a thermometer into the vat to
take the mixture's temperature and ensure the honey would
be the exact consistency desired when coating the model's
body. When the model was ready, an astonishing lunar body
plucked and powdered, hands, face, and cleavage covered in
white powder, the assistants went to work and began painting her with brushes, spreading honey all over her body,
one kneeling alongside her thigh with a short sable-hair
brush, another standing on a stepladder slathering her back
and shoulders with a roller, while still others smoothed the

honey over her flesh, daintily patting her skin with moist, delicate gauze compresses, and a cluster of young interns in white smocks circled her unmoving body with hair dryers to even out the latest layer and give the dress one last touch of lacquer. A dresser ran up with a pair of high heels and presented them to the model, who hoisted herself into them one foot at a time, leaning on the shoulders of crouching assistants even as they escorted her to the wings while giving her hair a final finishing touch.

And so, all at once as the music broke out, the model took off down the runway, followed by a swarm of bees that partnered her pace, trailing after her in an electric buzzing of thousands of insects that drowned out the onlookers' admiring exclamations. It was an unhoped-for success, the model had reached the end of the catwalk, paused briefly contrapposto, a hand on her waist, and then set off again the way she'd come, when the miracle happened, the swarm of bees pulled a pitch-perfect about-face along the exact curve of her course, floating in their broader turn beyond the runway over the heads of the audience, eliciting another round of admiring exclamations. This had taken less than half a minute, and the model was already retracing her steps when, just as she was about to reach the wings, she hesitated for a split second over the two exits available to her—stage right, and stage left—and, remembering her special instructions to head left so the bees could return to their hive, she changed her mind at the last minute and switched directions, and in that split second, that infinitesimal indecision, it all fell apart, came crashing down, the spell broke and she tripped onstage, collapsed on the floor, she felt the bees' loud breath fall at once upon the nape of her neck, and it was then, at that very instant, the hunting horn sounded, that the bees stung her all over, her back, shoulders, breasts, neck, eyes, her sex and inside it, the model curled into a ball on the floor shielding her face with her hands, struggling, fending off the bees' attacks with an impotent arm, getting up on her knees and fleeing on all fours, but falling again, vanquished anew, like a living torch, immolated, writhing on the runway, several people having dashed from the wings to her aid, horrified helpless assistants, the German beekeeper who'd burst out of nowhere like a Grand Guignol puppet, oafish and lurching, in his white spacesuit and thick gloves, wiremesh mask over his face, Japanese firemen, extinguishers in hand, who'd positioned themselves over the model but hesitated to start spraying for fear of making things worse.

That was when the curtain went up and Marie slowly made her appearance onstage to greet the public, as if it had all been part of her plan, as if she'd conceived this tableau vivant, the supermodel martyr surrounded by multiple faces frozen in pain, European faces, Asian faces, thunderstruck, slowed, stilled, as if in a Bill Viola video, while around the tableau's central figure, still crumpled on the floor beneath a swarm of bees, the masked and clumsily costumed effigies of the beekeeper and the firemen faced off, knees bent and extinguishers in hand, as if forever fixed in an interrupted act of rescue. For, refusing to be defeated by reality, Marie had shouldered chance and claimed responsibility for the image so completely as to throw the audience into doubt, as if the entire scene now unfolding before their eyes were the result of her premeditation. But little matter whether the scene had been premeditated or not, the image had arisen, in reality or in Marie's imagination, and she had taken credit for it: by making her entrance onstage, she had signed the canvas, had placed her seal on life itself, its accidents, its hazards and imperfections.

Until now, when working on a collection, Marie had always clung to what she could control, the tiniest details, so tiny they didn't even have a name, too infinitesimal to be put into words, the *details of details* that, in her studio, she could instinctively spot on a dress in progress with her expert eye and immediately correct, annotate with a line of pins, amend on her knees with undetectable alterations, fabric folded, pinched between her fingers, plucking needles from a pincushion, eliminating errors and fixing problems as they came up, endlessly nitpicking, new imperfections emerging in light of the latest corrections, and so on and so forth, to infinity. For what Marie sought was perfection, excellence, harmony, a certain accord between form and fabric, the fusion of hand and eye, act and world. Perfection, that mirage we pursue in vain, ever receding like the horizon, forever inaccessible, with every step still just as hopelessly far away, even if landmarks, fixed landmarks on the ground, show us how far we've come since the first draft, when the work was no more than a distant glimmer in the mind's misty limbo. But in her endless quest for perfection, Marie had never yet consciously envisioned working on what escapes us. No, she always wanted to control everything, never seeing that what escaped her might be what was most alive in her work. For perfection bores us while the unforeseen invigorates. The unexpected conclusion to the show at the Spiral made her realize that in this duality inherent in creation—what we control, what escapes us—it is also possible to act on what escapes us, and there is room, in artistic creation, to embrace chance, the unintentional, the unconscious, the fateful, and the fortuitous.

I

In early September, returning from the Isle of Elba after the great fire at the summer's end, we went our separate ways, Marie to her apartment on Rue de La Vrillière, and I to my little one-bedroom on Rue des Filles-Saint-Thomas, where I had moved after our separation. As I was getting out of the taxi (we'd shared a taxi from the airport in Roissy to Paris), I was unable to tell Marie how I felt about her—but had I ever been able to? Perhaps if there hadn't been someone else there just then (the driver waiting at the wheel to continue on to Rue de La Vrillière), I'd have been able to give free rein to my feelings at having to leave Marie after the two happy weeks we'd just spent on Elba. There was a brief moment of uncertainty, I gazed at Marie sitting in the backseat, I saw a mute question in her eyes, as if she were waiting for something—a final gesture, a confession—but I said nothing and simply reached my hand out. Gently, I pressed her wrist, at the same time giving it a goodbye caress. She smiled tenderly, with a glint of amused affection, and in a dreamy, undone, bewitching voice, said, "Just one touch from you, and mmmm . . ."

Little did I know at the time, but that was perhaps the last nice thing she would say to me for the next two months. Upon returning to the little one-bedroom on Rue des Filles-Saint-Thomas in the drab Paris gray that early September afternoon, all at once I felt demoralized, as if already anticipating the aimless days that awaited me. I set my bags down in the entrance, and did a tour of the empty apartment. Here and there, in the hallway, were piles of cardboard boxes I hadn't touched since moving in. The dark rooms smelled musty, a blend of dampness from outside and old summer warmth built up in my absence. In the bedroom, the bed was unmade, the strewn and rumpled sheets spreading in wavelets of white cotton. There was a pajama bottom lying on the floor and a bottle of mineral water still on the desk. I walked over to the window and looked outside. The street was empty. I stared into the distance, all the way to the Bourse, where the taxi whisking Marie away had just vanished.

I remained standing there at the window, staring at the wet street below, the sidewalks glistening with damp. A few passersby were wandering off under their umbrellas, and this familiar Parisian sight—Paris, gray, and rain—seemed especially jarring to me in light of the unbroken days of sun and azure we'd known for two weeks on Elba. I'd been in constant contact with Marie there, we saw each other all the time, we dined face to face on the patio, I brushed her bare arm in the hallways of the house and grazed her waist going down paths on our way to swim in the sea. Even if I never forgot we were separated, this separation neither pained nor weighed on me, since we were together all the time. This was the way, the only way, I now conceived of my separation from Marie, her being around.

In reality, I thought Marie would call me soon after she got home. I even imagined, just then, that in the next few days, Marie would suggest I move back in with her on Rue de La Vrillière. I knew that probably wasn't how she'd put it, but what I secretly hoped for was that things would happen naturally, and that, in the wake of our time on Elba, we'd see each other so often in the days to come, with such implicit pleasure and rediscovered tenderness, that one night, quite naturally, after dinner out, she'd suggest I come home and spend the night with her on Rue de La Vrillière, not to leave till the wee small hours of the morning. Then, as the days went by, this experiment would repeat itself, I'd leave later and later, until I was no longer leaving at all and bridged the gap, so to speak, bringing a few things from Rue des Filles-Saints-Thomas over to Rue de La Vrillière as needed, in short dreaming of an inverse move to the one I'd made at the start of the year when I'd come back from Japan, but slowly this time, in stages, progressively, shirt by shirt, book by book, one item at a time, instead of all my boxes at once, to make a clean break and clear out, as I'd had to do in the painfulness at the start of the year, when I'd called on a taxi van company to help me move.

I didn't dare admit it to myself outright, but what I was waiting for now at the window was—already—a phone call from Marie. I even hoped to get her call before stepping away from the window, before I had time to do anything in the apartment, go through my mail or unpack my bags, so that when I picked up I could say, the amused modesty in my voice perhaps tinged with a zest of triumph, "Already?" and the endless half-hour I spent in front of the window waiting in vain for Marie's call was like an abridged version of the two expectant months I was about to spend waiting for any sign from her at all. In the first few moments, fervor and impatience still held sway, feelings of love the days spent together on Elba had rekindled, the intact desire to hear her voice on the phone—perhaps intimidated, tender,

light-hearted, suggesting we see each other that very night—
and then, as the minutes, the hours, the days, the weeks, and
soon even the whole month of September went by without so
much as a word from Marie, my initial impatience gradually
gave way to fatalism and resignation. My feelings toward
Marie went progressively from the impatient affection of
those first few moments to a kind of annoyance I was still
trying to get under control. After a while, I no longer held
anything back and gave free rein to my resentment. Marie's
final act of fickleness, inviting me to spend two weeks with
her on Elba just to ignore me and not make so much as a
peep afterward, was but the ultimate demonstration of her
radical nonchalance.

But now a new element, perhaps, since our return from
Elba, was that Marie managed the feat of annoying me even
when she wasn't around. For up till now, whenever Marie
hadn't been around, I'd missed her immediately, nothing
whetted my love for her more than distance—what to say,
then, about her absence? This new annoyance, this more
deeply ingrained irritation, taking shape right there at the
window as I waited for her call, was perhaps the sign that
I was readying myself for our separation and imperceptibly
beginning to resign myself to it—except that, and here the
nuance is vital, it might very well be the case that if Marie

annoyed me so much *when* she wasn't around, it was perhaps quite simply *because* she wasn't around. There was also an odd, abiding element in my love for Marie, which was that as soon as anyone, even me, took it in mind to criticize her, and quite justifiably, with the best intentions in the world, I couldn't keep myself from dashing to her rescue straightaway, as in certain couples where the one defending his or her partner tooth and nail is in the best position to know the extent of that partner's shortcomings. In fact, I needed no outside detractors to come up with all the ill that could be said of Marie, I quite sufficed. I knew very well that Marie was exasperating. I knew perfectly well indeed, along with her detractors, who didn't even know the quarter of it, that she was superficial, fickle, frivolous, and careless (and that she never shut drawers), but no sooner did I alight on this litany of deprecating qualifiers than I saw the other side to these complaints, their secret underside, concealed from view, like the precious hidden lining of too-flashy finery. For though glittering sequins sometimes kept one from seeing Marie clearly at first, to reduce her to the frothy society gossip abubble in her wake would be to underestimate her. A more substantial wave, timeless, ineluctable, carried her through life. What characterized Marie above all else was her way of being in tune with the world, those moments when she felt flooded by a feeling of pure joy: then tears would start rolling uncontrollably down her cheeks, as if she were melting with rapture. I don't know if Marie was aware she contained, deep within, this unusual kind of exaltation, but everything in her bearing bore witness to her capacity for intimate harmony with the world. For just as there exists such a thing as oceanic feeling, so we may speak, where Marie is concerned, of *oceanic affinities*. Marie had a gift, that singular ability, that miraculous faculty, for being at one with the world in the moment, of knowing harmony between herself and the universe, in an utter dissolving of her own consciousness. Everything else about her personality—Marie the businesswoman and Marie the CEO, who signed contracts and closed real estate deals in Paris and China, who knew the dollar's daily exchange rate and followed the latest market fluctuations, Marie the fashion designer who worked with dozens of assistants and collaborators the world over, Marie the woman of her time, active, overworked, and urbane, who lived in luxury hotels and dashed through airports in cream-colored trench coats, belt trailing on the floor, pushing two or three carts overflowing with luggage, suitcases, clutches, portfolios, poster tubes, not to mention—dear God, I can picture it still—parakeet cages (fortunately empty, for she rarely transported living animals, apart from a thoroughbred—a trifle—as it happens, on her last trip back from Tokyo)—also characterized her, but only superficially, including her without defining her, encircling her without grasping her, nothing in the end but mist and spray beside the fundamental affinity that alone characterized her completely, the *oceanic affinity*. Intuitively, Marie always knew how to be in spontaneous tune with natural elements: with the sea, into which she melted with delight, naked in the salt water surrounding her body, with the earth, whose touch she loved, primitive and crude, dry or slightly slimy in her palms. Marie instinctively attained a cosmic dimension of existence, even if she sometimes seemed to spurn its social dimension entirely, and treated her every acquaintance with the same natural simplicity, ignoring age and formalities, seniority and etiquette, showing each the same considerate kindness, the same graces of sensitivity and benevolence, the charms of her smile and her figure, whether it was an ambassador having her over to dinner at his residence during a show, the cleaning lady she'd befriended, or the latest intern at the fashion house Let's Go Daddy-O, seeing only the human being in each of them without a care in the world for rank, as if, beneath all the finery of the adult she'd become and her standing as a world-renowned artist, it was the child in her that had survived, with that child's bottomless well of innocent generosity. There was something in her like a radical abstraction, an abrasion, a stripping-away of the social

reality of things, such that she always seemed to be wandering around naked on the surface of the world, the "seemed"
even being redundant with her, so often did she actually
walk around naked in real life, at home or in the yard of
the house on Elba, to the astonishment of creatures that
watched her rapturously, a butterfly coming upon its alter
ego in nature or the tiny, exhilarated fish quivering behind
her in the sea, when I myself wasn't the privileged witness
to her innocent fancy for walking around nude at the drop
of a hat, which was almost like her signature, her soul number, the proof of her integral harmony with the world, with
what has been most permanent and essential about it for
hundreds of thousands of years.

As we had just come back from Elba, these were the sunlit
images of Marie that now came to mind as I stood before
the window: Marie half naked under an old blue shirt of her
father's in the yard on Elba. I stared at the gray, rainy Paris
street before me, and it was Marie who raced irresistibly
through my mind without the slightest conscious effort on
my part. I don't know if Marie knew just how alive she was
in my thoughts at that moment, as if, beside the real Marie
who must have reached her apartment on Rue de La Vrillière
by now, where the taxi had dropped her off, was another
Marie, free, autonomous, separate from herself, existing only

in my mind, where I let her come to life and move about my thoughts as she went swimming naked in my memories or took shape in the yard of her father's house. I saw her again, then, in the little yard on Elba, that double, my personal Marie, wearing a basic swimsuit she'd pulled down and rolled around her waist because it was too hot (or even with no swimsuit at all, I kid you not). Cautiously, I drew closer to her in my mind, and through the tree branches in the little yard shivering in a light breeze made out her bare silhouette, the skin on her shoulder dappled with sun-shimmer, crouching by an earthenware jar, kneading the potting soil with both hands and tamping it down, evening out the earth around young shoots she'd just replanted and watered, watching the meager trickle from the hose intently, with a kind of meditative steadiness that seemed to wholly absorb her. I skimmed her shoulder as I joined her in the yard and told her in passing that for lack of a swimsuit, she could maybe put on a hat—people do that when they're naked, you know (and she shrugged, didn't dignify that with a reply). Marie, who always managed to surprise me, throw me for a loop, unpredictable Marie who, a few weeks earlier on Elba, had filched an apricot from the display at a fruit stand in Portoferraio's old town, and kept the pit in her mouth for a long time, sucking on it dreamily in the sun, before suddenly pinning me to the wall in a shady alley near

the port to press her lips abruptly against mine and dispose
of the pit in my mouth.

And then I realized that I was chewing over these same
happy visions time and again, the same summer images of
Marie kept coming back to me, as if filtered by my mind,
purified of any unpleasant elements and made more endearing still as they began to grow distant in time with my
return. But since, I told myself, any true love and, more
broadly speaking, any project, any undertaking, from the
flowering of a bud to the growth of a tree to the realization
of a work of art, has but one aim and intent, to persevere
in being, doesn't it always, inevitably, come down to chewing the same thing over? And a few weeks later, taking up
this idea again of love as rumination or continual reprise, I
would further refine my phrasing, asking Marie if the secret
to lasting love was never to swallow.

I don't know how much time had passed since I got back,
but day was beginning to wane in Rue des Filles-Saint-
Thomas, and I still hadn't budged from the window. The
street had gotten a bit livelier, a few signs were now lighted
near the Bourse. One of the houses across from me was
being renovated. On the fourth floor, an apartment had
been laid utterly bare, the façade gone, leaving the entrails

of the building exposed, as if after a hurricane or an earth-
quake. Under the arc lights, a few workers in helmets passed
to and fro over plastic tarps covering the floorboards of what
must once have been the living room. The scene had something, if not hallucinatory, then at least not very Parisian
about it (or I'm no Parisian), and seemed instead to be taking place in a major Asian metropolis, by neon light and the
glare of welding torches. I contemplated the building under
construction across from me, and thought back to the trip
Marie and I had made to Japan at the beginning of the year.
That was where everything had started, or rather everything
had ended for us, for that was where we'd broken up, that
was where we'd made love for the last time, in the room of
a luxury hotel in Shinjuku. We'd left for Japan together,
and come home separately two weeks later, each to our own
lives, no longer speaking, no longer bothering to stay in
touch. When I got back to Paris, I finalized our breakup, in
a way, by moving to Rue des Filles-Saint-Thomas, and we
had barely seen each other at all till late summer, when she'd
suggested I join her on Elba. But what Marie didn't know—
and still doesn't—is that I, too, was there the night her show
opened at the Contemporary Art Space in Shinagawa.

For there were many things Marie didn't yet know about the
end of my stay in Japan. When I returned to Tokyo—for I

went back to Tokyo after my brief visit to Kyoto—I got a room without telling anyone in a Tobu, a little chain hotel near the Shinagawa JR station. I spent three or four days alone in Tokyo, at loose ends, whiling away most of my afternoons on the bed of that hotel room. Since I hadn't managed to reach Marie by phone the night I got back, things had gotten inextricably knotted up for me, and I couldn't muster the strength or the energy anymore to try her again later in that empty room of the Shinjuku luxury hotel where she must have been waiting to hear from me. But since I knew the date her show opened at the Contemporary Art Space in Shinagawa, I resolved to find her there—without warning her, as a kind of surprise.

On opening night, I got ready in the little Shinagawa hotel room. I showered and shaved with care in the cramped bathroom. The mirror was fogged over, and I could barely make out my face. As I scraped rectangles of foam from my cheeks and neck, I felt like I was gradually finding myself again, surfacing after a long absence, a painful interlude in my life, a feeling reinforced by the fact that as the mirror defogged bit by bit, my face slowly reappeared in it, re-forming in fragments, like a puzzle being put together right in front of me, freeing first my eyes—my blue-gray anxious gaze—then my nose, my mouth, my lips, my chin. When my face was complete once more, shaved and seemingly reconstructed in its entirety, I set to studying myself. I gazed thoughtfully at my features in the mirror, curious, attentive, trying to espy what I was now feeling, a few hours before meeting Marie again after having vanished from Tokyo for several days without warning. I don't know what I felt—worry, the vague anxiety that hadn't left me since our separation?

I slipped on my big charcoal-gray coat and left the hotel room in the early evening. It was dark outside, the air cool but very clear, pure, transparent. I'd left the lights of the Shinagawa JR station behind me, and was walking down an ill-lit boulevard, bordered by a parapet, that looked like a city highway. Cars passed me by at high speeds in the dark, and I studied the cursory map I'd scribbled on a scrap of paper fluttering between my fingers, keeping an eye out for the left turn for the museum. That was when, in the distant gloom, I glimpsed the dark façade of the headquarters of a major Japanese company, and I had an astonishing slip of the eye, as I saw appear before me in the night SORRY, rather than SONY, in bluish neon letters along the building's pediment. I passed before the strange, silent writing on the wall, arisen from the city like a subliminal confession meant for Marie and, pushing forward still lost in my thoughts, I realized I'd gone too far, and wound up retracing my steps, heading for Gotanda. I don't know how long I spent going around in circles in that part of town. I'd lost my way, worry had taken hold of me, fear at having gotten lost on top of the anxiety I felt at the prospect of seeing Marie again.

A very lively atmosphere prevailed when I emerged into the parking lot of the luxury hotel adjoining the Contemporary Art Space in Shinagawa. A throng of taxis was pulling up and letting out passengers going to the opening, before pulling away again into the night in a slow-motion ballet of headlight beams, while other taxis pulled up solo, fluid glimmers rippling down the candy-colored metal of their doors. Official cars and a few limos were parked by a stand of trees, and gloved chauffeurs waited, smoking cigarettes in the shadows. A policeman tricked out in a yellow reflective vest was directing traffic by the service drives, guiding cars past angled barriers with slow waves of a lighted baton. All around, groups of guests were dawdling in the lot, in evening wear, invitations in hand, as at a concert or the opera, a few more eccentric outfits standing out here and there, colored glasses and gaudy hair, fluorescent scarves and dashes of hot pink. As some guests were already starting toward the entrance, and I'd begun to follow the drift, I went down the path toward the museum, head down, fearing the gazes of other guests, though I knew no one, and no one seemed interested in me. Snatches of conversation in all sorts of languages reached my ears, I caught bits of phrases out of context, incoherent fragments, comments cut off ("but that's exactly what I told him!"), or amusing ("*tu ne trouves pas, franchement, qu'il est un peu trop petit, mon chapeau?*"), or overlapping, incomprehensible ("*anata, jirojiro minaide kudasai*"), in English, French, Japanese (most languages left me cold, but whenever I heard a bit of French, I felt a sudden rush of anxiety, and hastened my step, or slowed down, to let the danger pass). The poorly lit path plunged deeper into the undergrowth, the slender silhouettes of trees could be glimpsed going down a gentle slope to a little lake. As we headed deeper into the dark, the sounds of conversation subsided, as if the shadows bade us lower our voices, and the last few yards to the museum were walked almost in whispers.

As we neared the museum, a constant murmur could be heard from over its high surrounding wall, a powerful, unbroken hubbub, voices ringing out more clearly, laughter, exclamations, and mingled with them, a few notes of music from nowhere filtering through, only to vanish nonchalantly in the cold night air. The twin metal leaves of the gate were wide open, and suddenly, in the night, the lighted shape

of the Contemporary Art Space in Shinagawa appeared,
its radical architecture in sharp contrast to the setting of
shadowy verdure that sheltered it. Traditional lanterns on
the ground traced a lighted path through the park, a hedge
of tiny living flames, amber and weaving, guiding guests
toward the main building. A hundred people or so were
making for the museum in a constant hubbub, their moving backs swaying in the tawny firelight. A gathering had
formed before the entrance, and young men in suits and
badges were checking invitations, directing certain guests to
a welcome table, where hostesses seated behind small cards
that said PRESS or GUESTS checked names off thick lists
several pages long, handing out individual envelopes and
catalogues. As I neared the entrance, I dissociated myself
smoothly from the crowd and slowed down. I loitered for
a moment, hands in my pockets, uncertain, head down.
Obviously I had no invitation, nor did I have any intention of introducing myself and having Marie notified of my
presence. I didn't even try to go in, I cast a furtive glance
inside, past something like an invisible barrier where two
young men with badges were keeping a watchful eye. For a
moment, I tried to pick out Marie in the hustle and bustle,
and I was as scared of catching a glimpse of her as of not
seeing her at all.

The museum's great black marble lobby was swarming with people, staff were collecting coats at the coat check. Freed from their coats, the women were revealed in evening gowns, bare-shouldered, fragile in the cold that made them shiver briefly from the draft and wrap their arms around themselves, pressing lightly with their fingertips, before hurrying toward the exhibit halls. I was still standing outside the entrance, and continued to observe the inside distractedly, when I spotted the glass booth of the surveillance room in a recess off the lobby. The door was open, and in the gloom a guard could be made out sitting before a row of security camera screens. The various monitors broadcast a mosaic of silent images, mostly frozen and heavily pixelated, sometimes flickering, slightly jerky. The upper row of monitors was focused on the park around the museum, as much on the path leading down to the lake, where guests coming down the path through the undergrowth could still be glimpsed, as on the great black marble lobby at whose threshold I stood. On another row, all the screens were showing images from inside the museum, but no precise details could be discerned, just a continuous swarming of undifferentiated crowds hastening toward the exhibit halls. I crept closer and started studying the screens, scrutinizing them one by one, carefully examining their surfaces, searching the electronic tapestry of monitors to try and make

Marie's figure emerge from the crowd—but there was no trace of Marie on the screens. Where was she, Marie? What did she look like tonight? What expression did she have on her face? How was she dressed? Marie the faceless. Marie the invisible. Marie, so absent tonight.

And yet I could feel Marie's unseen presence a few yards away, quite strong, powerful, magnetic, I could feel her presence in the museum, she had to be there, physically, in the exhibit halls, on the far side of the lobby I couldn't enter, perhaps secretly waiting for me, watching out for my arrival, and I couldn't do a thing, I couldn't reach her, I found myself barred by this symbolic border, this virtual roadblock nothing rational should have kept me from crossing. Nothing, that is, but the burning anxiety I couldn't shake.

That was when the guard with his back to me in the surveillance room turned around without thinking, his gaze met mine through the semi-opaque partition between us, an empty, distracted gaze, but I was immediately convinced he'd recognized me, even identified me, for he'd already seen me in the same big charcoal gray coat a few nights ago, when I'd gone to the museum after getting back from Kyoto and forced my way inside, a bottle of hydrochloric

acid hidden in my jacket pocket. I was convinced he'd recognized me and immediately turned around, escaping into
the night, taking off quickly toward the park's exit, lantern
flames flickering at my feet like so many fragile little flowers
tormented by the wind. I'd turned up my coat collar and
quickened my pace down the path without turning around,
passing a few late guests just now arriving at the opening,
shoving them aside with my shoulder, zigzagging, blazing a
trail, when suddenly I caught sight of the two red dots of the
security cameras atop the metal gates—and then instinctively I knew I was still on the screens in the surveillance
room, that the alert had been sounded, and that several
guards must have gathered in the security room to study
my progress through the park, tracking my figure with their
eyes from screen to screen. I changed tack abruptly then,
to exit the cameras' field of vision, to free myself from the
net of electric waves I was tangled up in. I left the path
and began striding away across the grass, moving toward
the edges of the park to skirt the museum. Catering trucks
were parked in the shadows by the service entrance to the
kitchens around back, and I slipped between the vehicles,
emerging in an ill-defined island protected by traffic barriers and garbage cans, filled with plastic crates containing
rows of identical brand-new glasses, boxes of bottles stacked
in piles, cocktail platters-in-waiting still covered in plastic

wrap. I came to a complete halt, not moving a muscle, holding my breath and pricking up my ears. Nothing, not a sound, I detected no trace of movement behind me, not a single crackle from the park.

I let a few more moments go by and then I began walking again. I made my way slowly through the dark, I'd slowed down to avoid obstacles, keeping one hand on the wall to guide me forward. That was when I was drawn by a sound, a vague murmur, actually, I couldn't tell quite where it was coming from at first. I looked up and saw light on the rooftop, hazy flashes of light no doubt from inside the museum. I examined my surroundings and noticed a fire escape going straight up the side of the building, enclosed by a cylindrical cage. Without a sound, I approached the fire escape and began to climb, taking care where I put my feet, clinging cautiously to the rungs, whose icy touch I felt beneath my palms. I felt my strength fading, my legs were giving out, my coat-tails were tangled up in my knees, hobbling my progress. The cold grew sharper the higher I went, a stinging little wind that seared my cheeks. I kept going all the way up the fire escape, until the sky above Tokyo appeared beyond the line of rooftops, very pure, a limpid black speckled with stars.

The roof of the Contemporary Art Space in Shinagawa stretched out silently before me in the dark, festooned with a dotted line of LEDs that highlighted the architecture of the building, shaped like an airplane wing. Pausing for a moment, I gazed at the necklace of blue lights—a creamy, cosmic blue, saturated with white—twinkling faintly in the night, sweet as starlight. I climbed the last few rungs of the fire escape and, with the help of one hand, setting a knee on the gutter, hoisted myself carefully onto the roof. I took a few crouching steps across the slightly sloped aluminum-clad surface without straightening up, keeping both hands on the ground, advancing in this stooped way past air vents that exhaled tentative ribbons of steam into the gloom. I could see the lights of Tokyo all around me, while the park below seemed to spread in a blind island of vegetation undisturbed by any artificial light. That was when I saw another opening on the roof, a little porthole that let out a white glow into the night. Cautiously, I made my way over to the source of the light, and leaning over the porthole, saw below me one of the exhibit halls where Marie's opening was taking place.

Crouching on the roof, I began searching for Marie in the crowd under the porthole, but I couldn't find her, all I saw was an indistinct mass of incomprehensible figures beneath me. I hadn't moved an inch, and my ears were pricked to catch the slightest sound from the park. Every infinitesimal variation in the absoluteness of the night, the slightest alteration in its immense silence, barely perturbed by the muffled hum of conversation I heard only as a muted murmur from below, made my heart beat faster. Everything was a threat to me, noises of course, the roof's metal cables cracking in the wind, but also the slightest movements of light I could sense in the darkness, the beams of headlights I saw moving in the night which, rather than moving away toward the horizon, seemed to be closing in on me almost inexorably. There I was, squatting on the roof, and continuing to look for Marie through the window, eager to find her as quickly as possible, knowing that I shouldn't linger, that I couldn't stay here indefinitely. My gaze fixed, intense, I quickly scanned the faces of the women at the opening, I widened my eyes, I strained my pupils. Sometimes, I'd think I spotted Marie in the crowd for a moment, convinced it was her from behind, among a group of guests, but when she turned around, I was forced to admit upon seeing her face that it wasn't Marie, it was a stranger, a decoy that had fooled me for a moment.

No one could have suspected that I was on the roof just then, but one of the guests suddenly looked up and almost caught me, forcing me to back up quickly from reflex. For a few moments, I kept my distance from the light before going cautiously back to the porthole, careful to expose as little of myself as possible to prying eyes, as if my body were a potential target and every look from below a weapon that might shoot me down. Now and again in the night, beyond the black line of undergrowth around the museum, the distant roar of a Yamanote Line train could be heard. I still hadn't moved an inch. My body held back—only the immaterial beam of my gaze plunged into the exhibit hall—I continued to scrutinize the brightly lit room below. It wasn't the first time I was seeing this exhibit hall, I'd already experienced it in the dark a few nights ago, unsettling, shadowy, ghostly, when I'd slipped into the museum after returning from Kyoto and walked swiftly through Marie's exhibit, a bottle of hydrochloric acid in hand.

Crouched on the roof, bent over the porthole, I tried to find Marie in the distant crowd milling about below. The noise of conversation seemed muffled by the thickness of the glass, and I wondered about the nature of the reality under my eyes. I wasn't sure how to gauge the nature of the benumbed reality that reached me as if through a cottony veil, this dulled reality which seemed something like the 3D projection of a scene from an abolished past, like one of those trancelike scenes generated by the invention of Morel in Bioy Casares' novella, a world nearby yet unattainable, on which I had no hold, with which I couldn't interact, the people seeming to mill about not in the present but in a past already over, in a kind of limbo—before birth, after death. I'd experienced this torn-between feeling before, while dreaming or reading, of finding myself in one place physically and somewhere else in my thoughts, in memories or the resurrected past, sometimes even in an imaginary elsewhere, not lived and reconstructed but invented from whole cloth, in an ideal world tailored to my liking, peopled by idle fancies and scattered with mental landscapes lit by my own hand. This dispersal of the self which, when we recollect the past, allows us to be here and elsewhere all at once, doesn't offend common sense so long as it's limited to movement through space. Only when we begin moving through time, and we have the feeling of being in the present and the past all at once—because memory no longer ranks and arranges different moments in time—does the mind struggle to find its bearings, because at such moments time is no longer perceived as the succession of moments it has always been, but as a superimposition of simultaneous presents. And, observing the activity in the exhibit hall beneath me through the porthole, I felt suddenly dizzy, for I realized that the present before my eyes resembled in every way a scene from the past, and it was only now, in the future, that I was becoming aware of it. It was only now, more than seven months later in Paris, standing before the window of my room in the little apartment on Rue des Filles-Saint-Thomas, that I had gained the necessary distance to apprehend all the elements of the scene then underway. But if so, where was I now? For wasn't I, too, like those quantum particles impossible to pin down precisely, if they're even anywhere at all at a given time, wasn't I in Japan and in Paris all at once, in Tokyo on the roof of the Contemporary Art Space in Shinagawa, watching for Marie through the porthole, and in Paris in early September, standing in front of my bedroom window on Rue des Filles-Saint-Thomas waiting for Marie's phone call upon returning from Elba? So where was I? Where—if not in the limbo of my own consciousness, freed from the contingencies of space and time, still and forever invoking the figure of Marie?

And that was when I realized it was that very night Jean-Christophe de G. had met Marie at the Contemporary Art Space in Shinagawa. So I must have glimpsed Jean-Christophe de G. that night—even if I didn't know him at the time, even if I'd never seen him yet and was unaware of his very existence—my gaze must certainly have fallen on him at one moment or another during the evening, which means I was—that I would be or had been—an eyewitness to their encounter.

In theory, Jean-Christophe de G. should not have gone to Marie's opening. The decision had been made unexpectedly that night after dinner, on the way out of a restaurant in Ginza, where he'd been invited by one of his friends, Pierre Signorelli. Massive, imposing even, his body and face ill-matched, the body of a rugby prop and the curly-haired, chubby face of a Tuscan pageboy—recalling more a portrait by Antonello da Messina than a self-portrait by his name-sake, Luca Signorelli—Pierre Signorelli was a fortysome-thing French businessman who had been living in Tokyo for over ten years. From his coat pocket he had pulled the cardstock invite, neglectfully bent in two, for the exhibit at the Contemporary Art Space in Shinagawa—an invite on elegant glossy cardstock banded simply with the title of the exhibit: MAQUIS, on a black background, echoing the title of Marie's show at Spiral, "Autumn Maquis," where her dress of honey had been presented—and he had shown it to Jean-Christophe de G., suggesting he tag along to the open-ing. Though utterly unfamiliar with the worlds of fashion and contemporary art, Jean-Christophe de G. (it was the first time he'd ever heard Marie's name, which appeared on the invitation in its most complete form: Marie Madeleine Marguerite de Montalte) had let himself be tempted by the proposition, and together, they'd taken a taxi to Shinagawa. Absentmindedly tapping his thigh with the invitation Pierre

Signorelli had handed him, Jean-Christophe de G. felt no particular curiosity about the exhibit, but the prospect of prolonging the evening on his first night in Tokyo was enchanting. He'd landed in Japan that very morning, but due to the time difference, he wasn't sleepy. His thoughts stimulated by the warm sake he'd drunk at the restaurant, a gentle warmth beat in his blood, spread down his veins, and rose to his brain, he felt himself filled with delicious well-being in the taxi's backseat. Through the windows, he watched the streets of Ginza parade by, the air was dark and clear, and life seemed rich with inexhaustible promise. Finding himself in Tokyo on the threshold of the evening's outing, he felt an unaccustomed lightness, a detachment, an insouciance. He felt like a conqueror tonight, and discreetly slipped off his shoes in the taxi's backseat to rub his stockinged feet voluptuously against each other.

The taxi had dropped them off in the parking lot of the luxury hotel adjoining the Contemporary Art Space in Shinagawa. With his first glance, smoothly exiting the car in the lot's muted glow, Jean-Christophe de G. had sized up the importance of the event, appraised the quality of the guests, and assessed the luxury of the cars parked in the shadows, black limos with gleaming fins, sometimes set off by a pennant testifying to diplomatic presence. Pierre

Signorelli limped along in his wake, short of breath, grunting beside him in his heavy coat of fluffy beige wool (a coat of considerable volume, which must have required the sacrifice of a whole flock of sheep or a good dozen camels). Listening only distractedly to Pierre Signorelli's explanations in his wheezing asthmatic voice, Jean-Christophe de G. directed tiny, piercing looks all around at the people walking with him toward the museum, and continued to gauge the guests with his steely blue eyes, judging the women's elegance, weighing the men's wealth, the value of their holdings. They stepped through the gates and entered the park surrounding the museum, which quivered in the flickering golden glow of lanterns. Jean-Christophe de G. hadn't yet set foot in the museum before he'd decided, as a secret challenge to himself, that he would emerge from it on the arm of this Marie, the artist exhibiting tonight, or if not on her arm, then in her company, that he would take her out for one last drink in Shinjuku and accompany her back to her hotel, or the night would end with the two of them in his own hotel (not every detail of the night was set in stone yet, a few gray areas remained, a slight vagueness he was willing to forgive, concerning as it did a woman he'd not yet laid eyes on, and whom he'd never heard of till today). There was no contempt in Jean-Christophe de G.'s nonchalance, just a whiff of daring, sport, adventure. His business was doing well, his self-confidence limitless. Women liked him, and he knew it. Not that he was particularly handsome, that wasn't the issue, but he was well-bred, intelligent, rich, and cultured. He knew how to be gentle, his gaze was firm, his hands soft. His charm was irresistible, just the kind of man of whom Marie would say, "I hate that kind of guy."

No sooner had he entered the museum than Jean-Christophe de G. had gotten rid of Pierre Signorelli, who'd soon become unwanted dead weight hindering his designs. He hadn't ditched him deliberately, no, he'd simply let Pierre dissolve in his wake (at one point he'd turned and Pierre was gone). Jean-Christophe de G. had checked his coat but kept his scarf, and he wandered through the crowd in a dark suit and immaculate white shirt, his scarf a blend of wool and black silk, watered with bright red glints, spilling nonchalantly over his shoulders. He made his way slowly through the crowd, brushing by stoles and bare shoulders, meeting women's gazes with his own, a tad too insistent. Busy with his thoughts of conquest, the veil of a delectable intoxication enveloping his temples, he had crossed the hall and made his entrance into the first of the large rooms where the exhibit was being held. But he hadn't looked at the works of art, the idea hadn't even occurred to him. He hadn't even spared them a glance, his utter lack of interest in the topic was sincere, unimpeachable. He maintained with contemporary art the relations of an enlightened amateur interested only in the market values of works (their price, the fluctuations of their stock), with an eye to possibly acquiring them without having to look at them.

The room before him was buzzing with a continuous hum of vague hubbub. Remaining on the doorstep, standing back discreetly, one hand in his pocket, he'd surveyed the room, eye sharp, senses honed. He had instinctively picked Marie out of the crowd, divined her unseen presence behind a kind of localized rippling, a pond of human ferment encircling a central figure still concealed by a dozen bare napes and jostling shoulders, on whom converged a bundle of gazes and desires, scattered, fleeting, fragmentary glimpses of outstretched arms and exhibit catalogues, cell phones held face-high in both hands to take photos, the circle finally opening like a sheet slipping slowly from stone to unveil a statue, and Marie had appeared before him for the first time, in an electric blue duchesse-satin dress. It hadn't been easy to approach her, but in stages, all calculated restraint and slipping past shoulders, insinuating his arm to clear a path through the crowd, he'd managed to join the tight inner circle pressing up against her. Spurred on by his savoir faire, he'd caught her attention and addressed her in French, their common tongue. Getting her alone for a brief moment's tête-à-tête was more complicated, but as soon as he managed, having plucked two flutes of champagne mid-flight from a passing tray, he'd gently toasted her, delicately clinking the two flutes together as if they were two hypersensitive epidermes touching for the first time, like two pairs of lips that draw close and brush against each other, an entirely token first kiss. Jean-Christophe de G. had achieved his goal. The only thing he didn't know is that the young woman he'd just toasted in such a promising way wasn't Marie (but everyone makes mistakes).

If you ask me, what must have led Jean-Christophe de G. astray was that the young woman he'd approached also spoke French, without the slightest accent, and her name was also Marie. But it wasn't Marie, it was another Marie (crazy how many Maries there are, really). As this Marie lived in Tokyo and knew everyone at the opening, she was one of the most popular women of the evening. The misunderstanding might have been quickly cleared up had Jean-Christophe mentioned in one manner or another the works Marie was displaying that night at the Contemporary Art Space—but he was careful not to, having absolutely no knowledge of Marie's artistic work—and if Marie herself wasn't talking about her work (and for good reason), Jean-Christophe de

G. believed it merely from modesty, which suited him just fine, for the subject wasn't one he really wanted to broach at the moment. He preferred to talk about himself, his reasons for coming to Japan, playing coy, modest, mysterious, keeping a low profile, not mentioning the nature of his many activities. He simply let Marie know he was in Tokyo for a few days as a horse owner, to see one of his thoroughbreds run a race at the start of the Tokyo Shimbun Hai that coming Sunday. In passing, brushing her arm in the course of the conversation, he invited her to come with him to the racetrack, and Marie who, it's true, was impervious neither to his charm nor the very determined manner with which he'd approached her, very direct, very deliberate, and at the same time was soothed by his fine manners and pleasing smile, had accepted with pleasure, won over by the combination of firmness and elegance emanating from his person (it's settled then, we're off to the races together next Sunday, at the Hippodrome de Fuchu).

Having thus managed to cut this other Marie off from the rest of the party, Jean-Christophe de G. hovered over her as if over a precious quarry, symbolically fanning his wings around her to prevent anyone else from approaching. In this way, they conversed in the thick of the crowd, laughing quite close to each other, gazes locked, bantering as they brushed each other's arms with their hands to punctuate their utterances. She often burst into laughter at his impertinent remarks, and even gave him an overdone little punch of protest on the shoulder, lips pressed tight as in a show of strength. Nestled up against her in the crowd, among laughter and polyglot exclamations, Jean-Christophe de G. leaned in to her ear to deliver gallant flattery. He made her laugh and told her anecdotes, and when she refused to believe he had a seahorse on him right then and there (which one might indeed reasonably doubt), he said he wished to surprise her but first required that she look away and, to make sure, he slipped a hand over her face to cover her eyes and, quickly digging into his pocket as if prestidigitating, he presented her, on the back of his hand, the promised seahorse nestled in a velvet box on a rumpled bed of cotton, with its pitiful, shriveled air of a wizened, pinkish chess knight. Marie's pupils gleamed with gratitude (as if it were the first time she'd ever seen a seahorse), and before her astonished delight, Jean-Christophe could not repress a modest smile of satisfaction, explaining to her as he wrapped the shriveled item back up in its wadding that it was a lucky charm for Sunday's race (my, weren't things getting interesting). And, knowing the stars were with him tonight, he took a deep breath and looked up in search of an opening that might let him gaze upon the skies over Tokyo, a witness to his triumph, and coming across the only porthole in the ceiling, he caught sight of my figure in my dark coat on the roof. My God, what the hell's that? he thought. Her husband? But barely dwelling on the thought—besides, I'd already vanished, he must have been seeing things—he grew lost for a moment in contemplating the skies over Tokyo, which could be glimpsed, limpid, in the porthole's perfect rondure.

During this time, Pierre Signorelli, who from sheer affectation hadn't checked his coat, was majestically strolling through the exhibit, hands clasped behind his back, in his muffler and heavy belted coat, as if conducting an inspection of a private residence, occasionally glancing at the works displayed along the picture rail with a measured and critical eye. When Jean-Christophe de G. saw Pierre appear before him, surfacing from the crowd, brow damp with sweat as if he'd just stepped out of the pool, though he'd stepped entirely from Jean-Christophe's thoughts and Jean-Christophe had forgotten he even existed, he was indubitably displeased by Pierre's reappearance and a veil of annoyance darkened his face. With his slow, complacent step, Pierre Signorelli came to join them. He kissed Marie's cheek in greeting and took her delicately by the waist, which threw Jean-Christophe de G. for a loop. A bit stung, but trying hard to keep a game face, he merely asked Marie how she happened to know Pierre Signorelli. Her smile full of mystery, Marie dodged the question and said that it was quite natural when they lived in the same city. Jean-Christophe de G. couldn't believe his ears (Marie also lived in Tokyo?). He didn't press the point. Pierre Signorelli's arrival had cooled his ardor, and he no longer said much, Pierre Signorelli was now the one keeping the conversation going, but since he wasn't saying much either anymore, there was no more conversation at all. The silence soon became a burden, awkwardness set in. They smiled at one another, embarrassed, looked around them. Immobilized, Pierre Signorelli, brow dotted with fine droplets of sweat that shone like dew on his skin, was sweating heavily in his thick coat, but he imposed this suffering on himself out of sheer vanity, no doubt secretly aware he cut quite a figure in that thick coat which must have cost him an arm and a leg. What do you think of the show? he finally asked. There was something of a rise, even an upsurge, in the level of awkwardness, a flash of panic in Jean-Christophe de G.'s eyes. Not exactly rocking my world, eh, said Pierre, and fell silent, saying no more. He lifted his head and looked at them, waiting for a confirmation. Jean-Christophe de G. was extraordinarily embarrassed—he even blushed—and without hesitating, owing it to himself to react, he felt obliged to rush to Marie's rescue. It'll surely be a hit, he whispered, pressing her forearm as if offering his condolences.

Surprised, Marie drew back, and looked up at Jean-Christophe de G. with an astonished and disapproving expression, as if he'd just committed not merely a faux-pas but a profanity (whether it was a hit or not wasn't really the issue). And since she hadn't yet given her own opinion on the exhibit, she gracefully swept back a lock of hair and began explaining that the works on display tonight were, if not commercial (in quotes, she said, scratching quickly at the air with two fingers from each hand to unite words and actions), at least a tad facile, a tad, shall we say, slutty (the adjective made Jean-Christophe de G. wince), and that on the whole, it was the same old same old, really very—very—superficial. Jean-Christophe stared at her incredulously, unsure what tack to take, and realized, thanks to this distressing incident—the unexpected arrival of Pierre Signorelli—that Marie had just transformed before his very eyes. Till now, she'd been largely a figment to him, the mere projection of a fantasy woman developing passively in his mind as he'd flirted with her. She'd never really reacted to his words, brought nothing personal to their conversation except her availability, her acquiescence, and her dazzling smiles. And now he realized that she was alive, that she had a personality, opinions, tastes, now he found himself facing not the blithe, seductive young woman he'd thought he was dealing with, but a fragile, tortured artist, possibly depressive beneath her blithe demeanor, at any rate inclined toward self-disparagement. Not exactly blowing me away, am I right? added Pierre Signorelli. No, not at all, said Marie pensively, after a moment's thought. Jean-Christophe de G. didn't know which one of them to look at.

At that point Marie, to soften the severity of her initial verdict, conceded that there were perhaps some pretty things (two or three worth saving, according to her), and Jean-Christophe de G. immediately clung to this last remark as if to a life ring, agreeing wholeheartedly (without specifying which works, of course). The three of them began drifting through the exhibit hall. They would move a few dozen feet in a random direction, nonchalantly, passing before works, pausing a moment. Pierre Signorelli would examine a photo with a kind of stubborn reticence, toying with the belt of his coat, which he wound idly in a loop before him. He'd raise his arm to point out the photo, rolling his eyes to get them to look, but saying nothing, simply sighing. Then he'd shake his head slowly, disapprovingly. Jean-Christophe de G. remained watchful at Marie's side, alert to her reactions, worried—she was so unpredictable—and finally wound up asking her in a low voice, with a great deal of respect, in a tone that simply attested to polite, well-meaning curiosity, where the photo had been taken. I don't know, Marie said evasively, with the barest of shrugs at the inanity of the question. No idea. She kept looking at the photo without looking at him. He looked at her (she was completely neurotic, no doubt about it). But Jean-Christophe de G. wasn't put off so easily. Come now, Marie, try to remember, he insisted quite tactfully, taking her arm. Look, I have no idea where that photo was taken, she said, freeing herself irritably (if you really want to know, go ask her, and she turned and pointed out Marie, far across the exhibit hall). And only then was everything clear to Jean-Christophe de G., who suddenly understood the situation, the misunderstanding he'd been bogged down in ever since the evening began. A powerful feeling of shame flooded him, he was mortified. The only thing that comforted him in his chagrin was that no one else seemed to have noticed his error. But, just as our relief at dodging great danger falls to pieces when we discover the true nature of the danger we've dodged, so Jean-Christophe de G., who up till then had surfed the crest of the misunderstanding with as much innocence as skill, suddenly felt off balance and vulnerable, in danger of collapsing, about to put his foot in it once and for all should he open his mouth. So he said nothing, all of a sudden he felt a great weariness and wanted to leave. He stayed there in silence, lost beside Marie, pained and pensive, darting desperate glances at the exit in the distance, as if casting about for an excuse to ditch everyone and slip out of the museum or even, if possible, to vanish from this story altogether, return to nothingness, from which it seemed he'd been plucked for a brief moment to beget, at his own expense, an evanescent ribbon of life, airborne, twirling, futile, and fleeting.

For a long time that night, once I'd reached the roof, I couldn't manage to spot Marie through the porthole. For a minute, maybe two—an eternity—I hadn't managed to pick her out of the crowd. I'd sought her out intently with my gaze, panicked by what I'd just done, by my own irresistible urge to climb the fire escape to the roof. And there I was, still hiding in the shadows, watching the exhibit hall through the porthole. One hand balanced on the aluminum cladding, I plunged my gaze into the exhibit hall in search of Marie. At first, I thought I'd only be up there a moment, ten seconds, maybe twenty, but I couldn't manage to find Marie in the crowd thronging below and I was getting impatient, afraid the museum guards, who might still be out looking for me, would spot me on the roof. At one point, behind me in the night, I heard the sound of something moving across the roof, and I spun around abruptly, but it was just the metal cables creaking in the wind.

I'd only looked up for a moment, but when I leaned back

over the porthole again, the exhibit hall, which until now had seemed an abstract space haunted by an unreal crowd, appeared to me in a more familiar light, and I made out the usual opening night crowd below me, several dozen living people flocking around art in an ongoing clamor of laughter and conversation. And if the scene seemed so clear to me, if it forced itself upon me with such a striking impression of reality, it was because Marie was there. Marie was there, I had her right under my eyes now, I could pick her out of the crowd, and she gave off something luminous, a grace, an elegance, an undeniability. She was wearing a white blouse with an ascot collar and floppy tie, not saying anything, but not letting anything show, not doing anything, not lifting a finger, not saying a word, not even blinking, she flooded the space with her unmoving presence, not cold, exactly, but aloof, faraway, unconcerned, as if lost in an exhibit not her own, seeming to tolerate with a resigned and deeply melancholy air the frivolities of these art openings, the superficiality of the conversations, all the fizzy spray which didn't even hit her, as if her skin were armored, her mortal coil steel-clad, and her soul simply a stranger to mediocrity, proof against vulgarity in all its forms.

I watched Marie in the exhibit hall, deeply moved, watched her poignant figure through the porthole and, my lips parted, I whispered her name softly in the night, though no sound came from my mouth, just a slight vapor, a hesitant breath that I saw idle for a moment before me, a little float-ing cloud of breath that had just meant "Marie" and was now dissipating slowly before my eyes in the cold night air. Then, slowly moving my lips once more as I watched Marie below, I told her I loved her—I said it on my knees. I love you, Marie, I told her, but no sound came from my mouth, I couldn't even hear myself say it, maybe I hadn't even opened my mouth, maybe I'd only thought it—but thought it I had.

No sooner had I spotted Marie than the anxiety that had been gnawing at me for several days suddenly disappeared. Marie wasn't saying a word, she seemed to be alone in the exhibit hall, she received the buzzing of compliments with indifference, staring into space, surrounded by a motley court of officials and admirers, and I perceived a fragility in her, a pain, a secret, subterranean rift perhaps tied to the breakup we'd found ourselves irreparably going through for a few days now. I never took my eyes from Marie through the porthole, and after a moment, from watching her so closely, I realized that I could read her lips, at first simple, summary utterances, natural punctuations that merely accompanied an easy-to-understand situation, as when I saw her greet someone and her lips formed the word "Bonjour," or when I managed to decrypt from the almost slow-mo, sleepy movement of her mouth, a muted "Nice to meet you" which she uttered wearily, nodding her head with discreet cordiality, or extending a reticent hand to a VIP who'd been introduced to her. I held my breath in the night on the museum roof and kept watching her through the porthole. Squatting in the shadows, I couldn't tear my eyes away from her mouth. With growing apprehension, my heart sinking, I focused on the movement of her lips and was afraid, watching unbeknownst to her like this, of suddenly chancing on some shattering revelation, a secret, a private piece of information related to our love or the painful circumstances of our breakup, but the only sentence I could read from her lips that night, the only complete and intelligible sentence I caught in the two or three minutes I was on the roof, watching her through the porthole (before leaving the grounds, coming down from the roof and going back to my hotel), in short, the only sentence that Marie spoke that night in my presence, with the lighthearted, sovereign honesty typical of her, something like a spontaneous impulse that suddenly, as if by magic, recalled to me the very essence of her personality, was, "Oh, when I'm depressed, I make myself a boiled egg."

II

When we came back from the Isle of Elba after the great fire at summer's end, I heard almost nothing from Marie for two months—and I finally left the window, where I'd waited in vain for her call. Not until two months later did she call me at last. It was late October, early evening, I'd just dined alone in the kitchen of my little one-bedroom on Rue des Filles-Saint-Thomas. When I picked up, I heard Marie's voice in the phone, saying a simple "Hello" and pausing, not talking right away—I heard her breathing, her silence—Marie, undecided, hesitant, not saying a thing and finally asking if we could see each other. I'd like to see you, she said softly, I have something to tell you, and she told me to meet her an hour later, in a café on Place Saint-Sulpice.

After hanging up, I stayed at the window for a long time, moved, disoriented, intrigued by the few words Marie had uttered. I thought a bit about the little she'd said, the little that had nevertheless contained an enigmatic "I have something to tell you," all the more puzzling since she hadn't said what. The void she'd left in the conversation—that lack, that absence—left room for all manner of hypotheses, from the most banal to the most tragic (a death, of course, since every time Marie had called me out of the blue lately, it had been to inform me of someone's death, her father's two summers ago, and Jean-Christophe de G.'s last June), and gave free rein to all kinds of conjectures, without lending credence to so much as a single one.

Emerging from the stairwell of the Saint-Sulpice metro stop into the night, I headed for the café where Marie had told me to meet her. Paris was very quiet that night. Most shops were closed, a few window displays could be made out in the gloom. Now and again a lone taxi would pass by in the rain on Rue du Vieux-Colombier. It wasn't very late, a bit past nine-thirty, but there was almost no one on the streets. Place Saint-Sulpice was empty, the church façade silent, swathed in majestic gray tarps that covered its immemorial scaffolding. An autumnal ambiance prevailed in the city that night, the bare branches of plane trees bowing in gusts of wind, a few fallen leaves wafting idly down the street, while others, crumpled, flattened, littered the ground among the empty benches. The café where we were to meet was practically the only lighted building in the square. Its golden glow could be made out through the glass partitions of the enclosed terrace, which looked like the bridge of a ship run aground in the night.

When I entered the café, Marie wasn't there yet, I was very early. There were no more than five or six customers scattered throughout. The windowpanes were fogged up, and there were multiple sets of wet footprints on the floor. Through the picture window, I watched the empty square before me, and every time a lighted bus stopped in front of the café, I couldn't keep from looking for Marie. I watched people get off and vanish down neighboring streets, and then I'd watch the bus leave, moving slowly off into the rain, toward the Seine or Les Invalides.

When I saw a taxi, a white Mercedes, slowly come to a halt in front of the café, I knew right away Marie was inside. I tried in vain to make out her face through the car's dark windows as she paid the driver, but I couldn't, nor did I recognize her immediately when the door opened, I even had a moment of doubt when I saw her step out of the taxi. I'd recognized her figure, of course, I knew it was her, but she had none of her usual flamboyance, her windblown look or her extravagance, it was a low-profile Marie who'd just shown up, like a toned-down version of herself. She pushed open the glass door to the café, looked around for me, and smiled shyly at me from a distance when she saw me across the room. She came over, gave me a kiss on the cheek without taking off a single one of the countless layers swaddling her from head to toe, and then slowly, she began to undo her scarf and remove her gloves, pull off the pompom beanie from which she shook a few droplets of rain that had humidified it as she was getting out of the taxi. She left her long dark coat on, letting the belt trail on the floor, and sat down beside me on a wicker chair, facing the window that looked out on Place Saint-Sulpice. She smiled at me again and shivered, hugging herself for a moment to stay warm. Beneath her coat, which she'd only opened halfway, multiple layers of woolens could be glimpsed, and she wore loose-fitting black pants with little laced-up leather ankle-boots. It had only been two months since I'd seen her, but I found her different. Perhaps because my feelings toward her had evolved since summer, I now observed her in a far more neutral fashion, scrutinized her with a more penetrating gaze, less immediately won over. She looked tired. She wasn't wearing any makeup, she'd lost the summer glow that lent her skin a wonderful apricot hue. Her tan had faded, giving way to a pale complexion and a sallow look. Her eyes were tiny, lifeless, pained, as if enfeebled by the too-bright café lights. Dare I say it even looked like—but no, of course not, I wasn't about to start with such a scathing insinuation—she'd put on a little weight, or rather, to soften the harshness of the affront, the outrage, the lèse-majesté, like something about her face tonight reminded me of how she looked upon waking, upon surfacing slowly from a long night, her sweet face still sleepy, lukewarm, her cheeks slightly doughy and her cheekbones unctuously puffy, which made her less pretty, perhaps, but more endearing.

Seeing her so tired tonight, her features drawn, as if wilting on the wicker chair, it was hard to imagine the meeting had been her idea. You'd have thought I was the one who'd called her up impromptu and forced her from her house without warning, jerked her out of bed or dragged her from the big sofa in the living room on Rue de La Vrillière, where she'd probably been lounging around, flipping through a fashion magazine, all curled up in socks and a shapeless old tee, a shawl over her knees, when my call had surprised her and she'd had to break off her evening reluctantly to come and meet me, quickly slipping on a pair of shoes and tossing on the first coat at hand over the baggy, comfortable clothes she was wearing when I'd disturbed her. Clearly she'd made no attempt to get ready for the meeting she'd requested. She'd barely done her hair before stepping out, and it was likely that late in the afternoon she still hadn't known we were going to see each other tonight. A waiter showed up at our table. I ordered another beer and Marie hesitated, hesitated quite a long time, her face raised toward the waiter, about to order but endlessly deferring her decision. Do you have any herbal tea? she finally asked. The waiter nodded and rattled off the available flavors—chamomile, lime-blossom, mint, verbena—and Marie asked him if they were fresh infusions. No, dried in bags, he said. I'll just have water then, she said, a bottle of Vittel. Evian, said the waiter. Evian, said Marie, and some chips if you have any, she added, as the waiter walked away.

The conversation with the waiter had revived Marie a bit, like a brisk shake, a quick warm-up, you could see her catching a second wind, and she straightened a bit in the chair. When the waiter came back with our drinks, setting the glasses and a small dish of chips down on the pedestal table, Marie's gaze settled pensively on the chips, and for the first time since she'd arrived I saw something like tenderness in her eyes. She laid into the chips, her mind elsewhere, and went through them all in under two minutes. She asked the waiter for more, and he hadn't yet left when Marie asked him if she could also have a few olives. And when the waiter came back to our table with a bowl apiece of chips and olives, Marie, who till then had still seemed somewhat less than her usual self, still a bit listless, a bit blunted, suddenly regained all her faculties. Marie became Marie again, and pulled out all the stops. Thanking the waiter for the olives, she caught his arm and asked him with a great deal of elegance, charming naïveté, and a disarming, complicit, irresistible smile, which seemed to say she knew she might be laying it on a bit thick, but you are who you are, a leopard can't change its spots, might it in any way be possible to have black olives, black ones instead?

Marie picked up her glass from the table and took a sip of water, a tiny one, reticently, pensively, almost without wetting her lips. She looked up at me, seeming to want to say something, but held back, thought it over some more, deeply absorbed in her contemplation. She took another sip of water just as slowly, staring fixedly at Place Saint-Sulpice outside in the rain, and told me Maurizio, the caretaker of her father's house on Elba, was dead, his son had just called to tell her tonight.

She turned and gave me a long, serious look, adding that it would be good if we went to the funeral. "We," she'd said, if "we" went to the funeral. I looked at her, and she fell silent, went back to watching the rain fall outside on Place

Saint-Sulpice. So once again, Marie had called me up to tell me someone had died (when all was said and done, she only called me up in the event of a death). Yet despite it all I was touched, even moved to note that at every important moment in her life, when something serious befell her, I was the one she always turned to. I would, without a doubt, have been even more annoyed to learn she'd gone to Maurizio's funeral on Elba without telling me first.

Marie kept gazing in silence at Place Saint-Sulpice, and I stepped away for a moment to go to the bathroom. When I returned, Marie had disappeared. I paused for a moment by the counter, Marie was gone, the table was empty except for what remained of our drinks, the beer I'd ordered and her glass of Evian. There was her absence, obvious, visible, undeniable. I looked around, I inspected my surroundings. Maybe she'd switched tables, or gone for a newspaper at the counter. I checked the other tables, but she wasn't there, I couldn't find her anywhere. I glanced quickly at the owner and the two waiters behind the bar, who didn't seem to have noticed anything peculiar, but I didn't ask them anything, my gaze fell on our abandoned table again, where the glasses and empty dishes testified to Marie's absence.

And that was when I saw her, glimpsed her through the café

window, she was sitting outside on a wicker bench, back against the glass, smoking a cigarette in the night, unmoving in the wind and rain. There she was, outside, at the edge of Place Saint-Sulpice, staring fixedly at its lights, cigarette in hand, arm slightly raised, wrist bent back, smoke rising very slowly in the air in tentative whorls, and I could see the red tip of her cigarette glowing brighter each time she took a drag. I could see her hair from behind, her hair matted in the wind and rain falling endlessly before her. Sometimes droplets spattered her face, and her long coat was soaked, as well as the scarf she'd put back on to go out. The neighborhood was empty that night, the rain was keeping people indoors, it was just us in Place Saint-Sulpice, me on this glassed-in ship's bridge overlooking the murky horizon, and her outside, a figurehead on the prow, facing the invisible ocean.

Place Saint-Sulpice swam beneath the streetlamps, and a few lonely points of light shone here and there in the offshore night. At the heart of the square, water overflowed the upper basins of the Visconti fountain in cascades, limpid, turbulent, swirling water lit by floodlight beams, tumbling from pools and bubbling up in the final basin where rain continued to fall, mixing water with water, while the imposing silhouettes of the Saint-Sulpice church towers rose to loom in golden-brown profile over the square. I gazed at Marie before me, catching fleeting glimpses of her features when she moved slightly, she kept staring straight ahead, cigarette in hand, her figure from behind in a coat in the rain, Marie the oceanic, who seemed to exhale splenetic vapors that dissipated in the night, borne away hither and thither on curlicues of smoke. Through the café window, I gazed at Marie's figure from behind—she was heartbreaking that night, in the rain—and I realized then and there, I just knew in a flash, that wasn't it, what she'd had to tell me—it wasn't Maurizio's death and the suggestion we both go to Elba for the funeral—but whatever it was she had to say, she hadn't yet and wouldn't do so that night, but only a few days later, on Elba. And later, I would think back to this very moment, and it would turn out that I hadn't been wrong.

Marie took care of all the formalities for the trip to Elba. She came to pick me up in a taxi the next morning. The taxi stopped in front of the building on Rue des Filles-Saint-Thomas around 5:30 a.m. (Marie had booked the first flight for Pisa, which took off at 6:55). It was cold and rainy in Paris, and we didn't talk much in the taxi. Marie was wearing a lightweight woolen coat, cream or ivory-colored, which I'd never seen before. She nodded off a bit in the dim taxi, arms crossed, bundled up snugly in her coat. Now and then she would yawn, close her eyes completely, then open them halfway and smile at me, eyelids heavy, ready to fall shut again. At Roissy, in an airport already bustling despite the early hour, we gulped some coffee quickly from plastic cups, standing at the counter of an express café after checking Marie's suitcase (just one suitcase—a miracle— but voluminous, and ingeniously endowed with compartments and appendices, subsections and added pockets, like one of those camping framepacks filled to bursting, with an ice axe sticking out and a saucepan dangling from the side). Then, once past the security checkpoint, we boarded the plane down a glassy gangway that overlooked the darkened runways of Roissy.

It was still dark when the plane landed in Pisa, the lighted terminal could be made out through the porthole. The plane rolled slowly down the runway of Galileo Galilei airport toward its gate. The local time was 8:35 a.m. and the temperature outside was 42°. We didn't dally at the airport, just grabbed Marie's suitcase and headed for the station. Checking the train times on a large display, we bought two tickets to Piombino and boarded a departing train that started moving almost immediately. A rainy day was dawning over Tuscany. We could see rough seas in the distance, gray and littered with tiny gashes of white spray, frothing

offshore like living, shivering scars. Damp, gloomy landscapes paraded by the window, train stations of washed-out
ochre, drizzly fields, and here and there, a solitary house
atop a hill, pines in single file distinct against the fog. Fall
didn't seem to have touched the foliage yet, still green and
without a trace of the yellows, golds, and russets to be found
further north in Europe. We dozed next to each other in
the train, as if slightly lagged from the mere fact of having risen so early that morning. As the train slowed just
before Piombino, nearing the station, we passed an iron-
works behind a chain-link fence, where tall industrial chim-
neys spewed smoke into the skies against the backdrop of a
dreary, grayish Mediterranean Sea.

The little station at Piombino Marittima lay at the end of
the line, a kind of railroad cul-de-sac that ended in the
port itself. We got off on the platform, and without leaving the building, climbed a stairway to the ferry terminal's esplanade. The terminal was practically asleep, a few
trucks lined up, drivers waiting by their cabs, cars of Italian
families headed to Elba for All Saints' Day. We made for
a glass-paneled building that said Agenzia Marittima and
bought tickets for the crossing, then went to await the boat
on the quay. The sky was very dark, the seas rough and
stormy in the distance. From time to time, a wavelet would

spill over the port basin, splattering our shoes. There we were, Marie's suitcase at our feet, looking at the two large, docked vessels that loomed unmoving before us, the azure blue of the Moby Lines ferry with MOBY painted in massive letters on the hull, and the more tumbledown Toremar, which we were going to take, its funnels already pouring out smoke in anticipation of departure. We were watching the final preparations for boarding, the metal barricades the staff moved aside to let vehicles aboard, when Marie gently took my hand in the rain. She hadn't looked at me, simply lifted the hand that hung beside her and taken my own quite naturally, and this gesture, so unexpected, so tender that it filled me with calm, couldn't have surprised me more had the two ships before our eyes relinquished for a moment the impassive froideur with which they shared the port, and suddenly drawn close to each other in a gesture of tenderness. I felt Marie's damp hand against my palm, and right away I physically savored, as if in a wholly private way, the application of that universal physical law by which two bodies entering into contact with each other will tend to reach thermal equilibrium.

The seas were rough that morning, and the ferry began to pitch as soon as we left port. The poop deck was deserted, swept with rain and spray, the benches outside abandoned in the wind. I propped my elbows on the railing and watched the heavy, rolling seas the ferry plowed through in the rain. The crossing lasted less than an hour. Soon the shores of Elba could be glimpsed in the distance. The air was blurred with rain, we could barely make out the wooded shores lost in damp fog. And yet the sight of approaching Elba by boat was a familiar one, though I'd only ever made the crossing in the summer, on calm seas in the marvelous liquid pink morning light. Today, it was hard to tell sea from sky, the coast seemed untamed, with scraps of mist clinging to every rocky outcrop. I watched the even line of the hills on the horizon, and realized just then—I hadn't noticed at first, so completely did the smoke blend in with the clouds—that a column of smoke was rising from the Isle of Elba.

The closer we drew to shore, the less room there was for doubt, it was indeed smoke we were seeing in the distance, as if the Isle of Elba itself were on fire. It was so striking that it seemed to me the same fire as last summer, even if that was no doubt impossible, the same forest fire now finally winding down but still burning, and pursuing us, awaiting our return. At summer's end, we'd left Elba in flames, and found it in flames again two months later. Soon the faintest smell reached us offshore, thinned-out, watered down in the marine air, not really the smell of fire, a forest fire, but just a burning smell, more acrid, more rubbery, floating in the atmosphere and scattering in the wind and spray.

The column of smoke was now clearly visible on the horizon, we could make it out quite well from the boat. It was fairly narrow at the base, broadening as it rose skyward, where it mingled with black and blue cloud formations, swollen masses of cottony cumulonimbus moving slowly in the wind. I was trying to pinpoint the source of the column of smoke when I realized it was likely not the city itself, but a locality slightly further east along the bay. As we neared the rocky promontory that marked the entrance to Portoferraio, the engines slowed, and the ferry drifted slowly forward till it drew abreast of the quay.

Marie had told Maurizio's family we were arriving that morning, and one of his sons was to come pick us up from the ferry and drive us to Rivercina. Maurizio had two sons: Francesco, the elder, who was a tax collector, and his younger brother Giuseppe, whom I barely knew, I must have caught a glimpse of him once or twice though we'd never really talked. We left the ferry through the hold, we didn't know who was coming to pick us up, and we looked vaguely around the quays. Marie instinctively headed for the little port authority building, where her father used to wait for us, and we saw that a pickup truck was waiting in the gray day, a huge black pickup with fat, gleaming fenders, motor running, headlights on in the rain.

Giuseppe, Maurizio's youngest son, got out of the pickup, dressed in black from head to toe, maybe because he was in mourning, but they could also have been his usual clothes, a black silk shirt, a thin faux-leather jacket, black Ray-Ban-style glasses, which he removed when he reached us, face unreadable and eyes staring straight ahead, not a word or a smile. Two glints of gold brought out the black of his outfit even more: a thick golden wedding ring, visible on his finger, and a heavy chain bracelet, gold or gold-plated, with his name, *Giuseppe*, engraved on it in elaborate cursive letters. He gave off a disagreeable and unpleasant air, he looked just like his car, the way some dog owners always wind up with filthy creatures that look just like them. Marie hugged him, put a hand on his shoulder and offered her condolences, quickly giving his hair an affectionate, messy ruffle. *È la vita*, he said without conviction, somewhat weary, even bored, and came toward me, briefly hesitant about letting me hug him too, though I had no intention of doing so, I was fine just sticking out my hand and keeping my distance. He shook my hand resolutely, unsmiling, determined, grip firm. I said something nice about his father in Italian, said

I'd always liked the man and everyone in Rivercina had loved him, and nodding as he listened to me, fiddling with the keys to his car, he said the same thing as before, "*È la vita*" in the same bored tone, as if he'd already said it a hundred times today, and would say it a hundred more.

Giuseppe eyed Marie's massive suitcase, hoisted it just like that as if it weighed less than ten pounds instead of the sixty it must have, and headed for the back of the pickup, whose bed was covered with a thin aluminum top that kept it sealed tight. He opened the gate with his keys, did a bit of tidying up so the suitcase would fit, pushed back a few unopened cans of paint, plastic tubs, rollers, lifted an old plaid blanket, revealing two jerrycans, which he covered up again almost right away, putting the blanket back in place, then lifted the suitcase and slid it into the bed. We took our seats in the cab and he started off slowly from the port, Marie seated between us, hemmed in beside me on the only passenger seat. Giuseppe had put his dark glasses back on, and he drove in silence. Marie made conversation, asking after Maurizio's family, and he replied laconically, precisely, without pointless embellishment, in his bored, slightly weary way. Then, seizing on a pause in the conversation, I asked him where the black smoke we'd seen from the ferry was coming from. Staring straight ahead, without turning, he said the Monte Capanne factory had burned last night. *La cioccolateria?* said Marie. *Sì, la cioccolateria*, he said.

The Monte Capanne chocolate factory was about eight miles from Portoferraio, not far from the hamlet of Schiopparello, on the site of the former Prati cookie factory. Sometimes Marie would stop by in the summer on the way to Rivercina and buy a few bars of artisanal chocolate from a little retail counter by the kitchens that was open during tourist season. Sometimes I would go into the shop with her, and while she was picking out the latest flavors in fashion from the lineup, pink peppercorn, basil, or ginger, each bar lovingly wrapped in its ritual foil and slipped into a see-thru sheath adorned with the monogram MC, I would wait for her, peeking into the kitchens through a picture window in the shop, decked out with illustrated panels depicting the different stages in the making of chocolate. This family business on Elba still made chocolate in the traditional way, with old-model winnowers to crack the cocoa beans and antique rotating drums to roast the hulled nibs. The nibs were then conched between millstones and metal grates turned by rolling cylinders. The dozen or so people who worked there wore white smocks and hairnets on their heads. In the heat, the creamy cocoa butter oozed down the sides of the vats, seeped and trickled, syrupy, resulting in a fragrant, almost liquid chocolate liquor which was mixed in the kitchens with other raw materials involved in the making of chocolate, cocoa butter, sugar, vanilla, and milk products, depending on the type of chocolate desired.

The fire in the chocolate factory had started around four in the morning. It had first swept through the depots where supplies were stored, bags of sugar and cocoa beans, and from there, it had spread to the main body of the factory, to the kitchens and offices. A good forty firemen and no less than six trucks from Portoferraio, but also other fire stations on the island, had rushed to the scene, and the fire had only been corralled around eight in the morning. Even now, it was not yet completely under control. When Giuseppe had passed by half an hour earlier to meet us at the port, a good twenty men were still on the scene, trying to secure the place. As soon as we passed the traffic circle by the cement works on the way out of Portoferraio, the smell of fire, which we'd first noticed that morning out at sea, assailed us once more, that burning smell which now permeated the inside of the pickup despite the windows being closed, and which we could not ignore, which flooded the space, all-pervading. But this burning smell, vague at first, which I'd simply noticed without being able to define, had begun growing clearer in my mind ever since I'd found out it was a chocolate factory that had burned down, and with the help of this clue my mind managed to take its measure, reconstitute and refine it, wrap around it completely, until I could even detect sweeter, almost sugary notes in it, such that in my imagination an actual chocolate aroma was born, subjective and velvety smooth.

The air ahead of us darkened as we drove, and the road grew dimmer, as if we were driving toward night, toward the setting sun, rather than merely eastward. Wisps of smoke still loitered over the road, merging with the rainy mist we could make out through the pickup's broad, wet windshield, where the wipers came and went. A few miles further on, traffic had slowed, a selective roadblock had been set up, policemen directing traffic with the help of motorcycle cops in leather and cumbersome white helmets, we spotted their powerful motorcycles parked on the shoulder. Giuseppe had joined the line of cars and was making slow progress, both hands on the wheel when, overtaken by a sudden impulse, he swerved left and began heading briskly down the middle of the road before turning at the chocolate factory. Right away, several carabinieri ran up to him, and he rolled down the window. He exchanged a few words with them, quickly, curtly, I couldn't really understand what he was saying, and one of the carabinieri motioned for him to come forward,

cleared a path for him, and he passed through the factory
gates, kicking the pickup into gear down a gravel path,
speeding up to free his wheels from the muddy ruts where
they were getting bogged down.

He parked the pickup in front of the ruins of the building,
by a police vehicle and a few fire trucks. Without a word,
without a single explanation, he got out and we followed
him, uncertain, squelching around in the mud, dozens of
yards of tangled fire hoses still lay deserted on the ground.
Behind the nonexistent door and the shattered windows of
the little shop we knew so well, we could make out black-
ened walls and collapsed stonework. There were about
fifteen people in uniform, firemen, carabinieri, scattered
around in small groups, crime scene techs in their curiously
sterile outfits, white jumpsuits and antiseptic masks, who in
other circumstances could have been mistaken for employ-
ees of the chocolate factory. Everywhere across the esplanade
drowning in hundreds of gallons of water that had gushed
from the hoses, floated or drifted, upside down or in heaps,
plastic chairs, metal carcasses, charred debris. The smell here
no longer held any subtle notes, it was simply oppressive,
unbreathable. Whitish smoke was still pouring in a continuous plume from the main building with its collapsed
roof, while here and there steam kept rising slowly from

several fumaroles of heaped metallic debris. A few carabinieri had established a vague safety line, banning access to
the buildings, which weren't yet secure. We took a few steps
forward, lingering for a moment by the door to the kitchens. The walls were gone, there was nothing left but the
building's metal framework and charred roof beams, and
there, spectral, in the shadow of the desolate hangar before
our eyes, rose three stainless steel chocolate vats each almost
twelve feet tall, whose cylindrical walls had stood up to the
flames quite well, retaining their original color, gleaming
with a silver sheen in which the flames that had licked them
were fossilized in long brownish trails. All the rest had been
reduced to ashes and jumbled piles of charred rubble on the
ground: an upended conveyor belt, the ruins of an old Carle
& Montanari dosing machine adrift in the wreckage.

We only stayed there for a moment, but the whole time we
were at the scene of the fire, I'd been intrigued by Giuseppe's
little game, for rather than wandering around like us, disoriented, in the factory's ruins, he seemed instead to know
the place like the back of his hand, to know exactly where
he was going, I even saw him walk into a shed the fire had
spared, vanish for a moment and then reappear again, hands
busy as if quickly stuffing something under his jacket. I
was walking with Marie among the smoking mounds, and

would discreetly turn from time to time to watch Giuseppe furtively, always finding him in animated conversation with a policeman, the same plainclothes policeman (with an orange armband on his jacket sleeve), whom he followed past the carabinieri's barricades, entering forbidden areas, leaning over to study the statements with the crime scene techs. When we went to rejoin him, he didn't say a word, didn't smile, offered no explanation, made no comment. He went back to the pickup, then we got back in, and we all hit the road. As he was leaving, he waved at the policeman, and went back down the dirt road scored with ruts and tire tracks in the mud.

We were back on the road to Rivercina. Giuseppe had taken off his sunglasses, which he put in the glove compartment, and he drove in silence, lost in thought. He turned to Marie and stole a glance at us, no doubt we were but a single entity to him, a single two-headed bizarrely conjoined creature beside him on the passenger seat. He studied us with that bored, stubborn look mourning lent him, or maybe he'd always been like that and mourning had simply reinforced it, legitimized it, and having thus sized us up, he told us it was no accident. As he got no traction, he added, sneaking another quick glance, a glint in his eye—of defiance but also nasty satisfaction—that it had been arson, that the police had found evidence the warehouse doors had been forced, the locks jimmied. He told us all this in his bored voice, as if grudgingly, not looking at us, yet unable to hide a dark, grim satisfaction, the morbid pleasure that comes from announcing bad news when circumstances allow it—and they clearly did so all too seldom for his tastes—or stirring up painful things, wallowing in tragedy and resentment. Sitting beside me on the passenger seat, almost on my knees, lopsided on the seat, sidesaddle if you will, Marie watched him closely. He kept talking, and she watched him with a stillness that had grown imperceptibly even more still, more strained, more pronounced, a stiffness in her body which I could now feel more against my thigh, she had moved almost instinctively away from him and drawn closer to me, listening to him coldly—her stare fixed, disapproving— unsure she wanted to understand what he was saying, what he was trying to insinuate. Perhaps due to the obstacle of the language, we couldn't grasp all the nuances of his mono- logue, perhaps we were dramatizing harmless words, per- haps we were reading too much into what he hadn't or had barely said, in his allusive and venomous Italian. What he was implying, at any rate, was that the Scagliones, the fam- ily that owned the Monte Capanne chocolate factory, had thought they could do without paying protection money.

As we came within sight of Rivercina, Giuseppe, taciturn once more, slowed at the intersection for the little private road that led to the property. When we passed Maurizio's house, with its shutters closed, Marie leaned out the window to study the homestead with an expression of misty tenderness and sympathetic pain. She wanted to stop for a moment and give Maurizio's wife Antonina a hug, but Giuseppe, not heeding her request, not even stopping, in fact accelerating, spinning the four-wheel drive in the muddy road, said his mother was tired and didn't want to see anyone, Marie would see her that afternoon at the funeral. This was said in a clear-cut way—and brooked no reply. Marie gave him that same fixed and disapproving stare, but she didn't put up a fight, she knew she'd get nothing from him that he didn't feel like giving. And what he felt like just then was dropping us off in Rivercina as fast as he could and driving off, apparently he had more to do before the funeral. At the end of the road, we emerged into a kind of raised clearing with a lean-to where the old truck that had once belonged to Marie's father wintered among abandoned farm equipment. The road stopped there, and Giuseppe dropped us off at the top of the stairs, this was as far as he went, he handed Marie a bunch of keys to Rivercina, along with the big golden key to the house. We got out of the pickup, Giuseppe got out with us to help with the suitcase. When he opened the rear

gate, I caught another glimpse of the old plaid blanket on
the truck bed, and I knew very well, from having seen them
while Marie's suitcase was being loaded, that there were two
jerrycans full of fuel under that blanket. I'd even noticed
that no sooner were they in the open air than Giuseppe had
covered them up (as if to hide them, I'd even thought fleet-
ingly). And though I'd glimpsed those jerrycans for just a
few seconds, I remembered very well how they looked, two
red five-liter polyethylene jerrycans with black caps, which
at first I'd merely thought Giuseppe must use for his maintenance work, or for backup fuel for his truck, or maybe even
his boat—but which, upon reflection, might just as well
have been used to set fire to a factory.

Giuseppe left almost immediately. He got back in his pickup
and left us without another word. We started down toward
the house. Upon sight of the house silhouetted in the rain at
the end of the wooded path, I was struck by how completely
different it looked from the one we knew at the summer's
end, as if the change in season had taken place here rather
radically, without any of the tiny invisible transitions that
usually ease one season into the next. With the big golden
key, Marie unlocked the double-leaf door and pushed open
one side, which screeched as it scraped the floor. There was
not a sound from the foyer, nor any light. We made our

way through the dark, into the living room, and found a heap of lawn furniture which had been brought inside for the winter. The great black wrought-iron table from the patio sat enthroned in the middle of the room, with its heavy wrought-iron chairs stacked one atop the other. Folded umbrellas leaned against the wall, deckchairs stood upright against the bookshelves. Every shutter in the room was closed. It smelled of mildew and damp dust. Marie leaned over to turn on a little green lamp on the floor, and in the circle of that loosely plugged-in lamp, which flickered a few times before coming on, we saw the house's original furniture emerge, the wing chairs, the sofa, the oak desk that had belonged to Marie's father, which materialized in the greenish gloom covered in great white sheets and thick fluffy gray blankets. I cleared a path through the maze of furniture and into the room I'd stayed in last summer. The door resisted, didn't open all the way, blocked by other lawn furniture and an old barbecue that had been stored there. In the room, the bed was unmade, the box springs bare, with twisted, misshapen bolsters lying against the wall. I slipped past to the window, tried to push the shutters open to get some light, get some air, but the shutters resisted, and I realized, upon making my way back out of the house and around the outside, that they'd been boarded up for winter, a plank of wood had been nailed across them, and they were now impossible to open.

Marie hadn't moved, she'd remained in the doorway to the living room, staring uncomprehendingly at the heap of furniture, hands shoved deep in her coat pockets, speechless, overwhelmed, as if she'd just discovered flooding or a collapsed ceiling. I suggested we at least take the coverings off to get a better sense of the room. She let herself be guided, as if in a trance, helped me pull the big white sheets off the furniture. Then we took a few deckchairs out on the patio, moved the umbrellas. We made our way back and forth through the room, giving the house a more habitable look. I'd managed to open one of the rare shutters in the living room that wasn't nailed tight, and put on an old CD we used to listen to last summer (Lucio Battisti's *Ancora tu*). *E come stai? Domanda inutile. Stai come me e ci scappa da ridere. Amore mio ha già mangiato o no. Ho fame anch'io e non soltanto di te.* Marie smiled at me then—her first smile that day, maybe the only one (there was every reason to be pessimistic).

When it stopped raining, I went out to have a look around the grounds. I walked around the house and spotted a little garden behind the blue fence. It had fallen into decay, overrun by weeds. I didn't try to go in, I just went on my way, I struck out toward the shore. The ground was wet, the leaves everywhere slowly dripping rain. I passed the horse pen, empty in the gray day, with a few toppled fence posts, and went down toward the sea past deserted patios. I'd reached the edge of the property, and took a small overgrown trail that vanished into the maquis. The house was no longer in sight, and I was pushing on through the brambles and the brush when I heard shots in the distance, two, then three, like doors slamming in the immense silence of nature. I slowed down, I stiffened, pressing on but keeping a close eye on the motionless ridge of drenched shrubbery to one side. It must have been hunters, maybe poachers, what did I know. I kept moving forward, slower now, nervous, on my guard, expecting an unwelcome encounter, slowing down even more when I came out in the open, afraid of being taken for a target, deliberately making noise, coughing ostentatiously to attest to my presence and not be taken for game. When I heard shots again, two then three, maybe four this time—invisible as ever—but which I could tell were nearer now, more menacing, I hurried up the path back to the house.

When I returned, the front door was still open, I found Marie's suitcase in the same place where we'd left it. Marie hadn't budged from the living room, she'd turned off the music and was sitting in the big wing chair. I joined her in the living room and sat down across from her in her wing chair's exact twin. We didn't say a word. There we were, the two of us, sitting in our coats in the empty living room of this deserted house. The room had more or less recovered its usual look, though it was still quite dark and gave off a strong musty odor. I checked the time. It was a little after noon, Maurizio's funeral wouldn't start before three. The front door to the house was still open, and we heard the rain falling outside—the rain, uninterrupted, gurgling in the gutters.

Marie got up to pick out a book from her father's library, and began reading across from me. I watched her in silence. I could tell that she was gradually reclaiming the place where her father had lived, the rooms he had occupied, where he'd worked, where he'd read in the winter when he stayed in for long days while outside the rain fell without end. Marie's father had spent his final years in this house, surrounded by books, rarely stepping out, avoiding company. A cultivated man who spoke several languages (though not with anyone anymore), he had, little by little, cut himself off completely from the world. I could tell that for Marie, Maurizio's death had painfully reopened the wounds from the death of her own father. Here, in Rivercina, Maurizio's death was no longer an abstraction, news from far away, as it had been in Paris when she'd first learned of it. No, Maurizio had lived here, Marie had run into him every summer in this place for more than twenty years. Just last summer, she'd still seen Maurizio crossing this room with his sturdy, heavy step, to get to a bedroom or go upstairs. She must have been seeing him now at every age of his life, in the living room or around a bend in the hall, with his furrowed skin, broad shoulders, thick hands, almost always dressed in a coarse white-and-blue checkered shirt. Marie must also have had memories of Maurizio I couldn't imagine, inevitably, inextricably intermingled with memories of her own father in this very house. For here, in the empty living room of this abandoned house, her father's absence made itself strongly felt all over, palpable in every particle of air. Each object, each piece of furniture indelibly bore traces of his former presence, the library most of all, the impressive library of art history and philosophy he'd patiently assembled over the course of the years. Marie stopped reading and looked up at me, book in hand. She seemed sapped of all strength, adrift, spent, discouraged, unable to read, unable to do a thing. She smiled gently at me, and I saw a call for help in her eyes, for assistance, something beseeching, an immense weariness, discouragement, renunciation. I feel like crying, she said. I went over to her and she took my arm, pressing it to herself for a moment with poignant intensity. Using my arm, she pulled herself up, embracing me for a silent moment in the living room, in a gesture of unspoken gratitude for having come with her to Elba, of shared sympathy, as if we were offering each other our condolences for Maurizio's death, and perhaps, to a larger extent, the death of her father. It was chaste, restrained, unexpected, we were in our coats in the living room and held each other almost without touching. It only lasted a moment. Then she gently broke away from me and, re-energized, pulled herself together, and we headed toward the foyer to take her suitcase up to her room.

I followed Marie with the heavy suitcase, dragging it along behind me up the stairs. On the landing, we plugged in a night light and went down the hall to Marie's room. She went in first, I followed with the suitcase, and I saw her freeze in place, petrified, paralyzed—not a sound, not a gesture, perhaps a slight trembling, but she hadn't taken another step, she'd stopped short, lost all momentum, and was no longer moving. In her absence, someone had been sleeping in the room. The bed was undone, the sheets rumpled. I remained frozen behind her, just as surprised, as dumbfounded as she was, riveted by the unkempt blankets trailing on the floor. I glanced around quickly, there were a pair of fatigues balled up at the foot of a chair, an upside-down pair of huge clodhoppers. I saw an open bottle of water, notebooks on the floor, an ashtray filled with butts.

Marie started trembling, she was shaken on the spot by a brief fit of trembling, then she pulled herself together and said, "We're not staying here." It was irrevocable, definitive, and instantly she got a hold of herself, firm, determined, she was already going downstairs, resolved to leave the house. I'd barely had a chance to look around, check out the bathroom, inspect the drawers, opening and shutting them hastily after a quick look inside, when in the lowest drawer, among some sheets and Marie's things, I came across some ammunition, boxes of bullets. Carrying the suitcase, I hurried down after Marie, she'd already gone into the kitchen to grab the keys to her father's truck, and was waiting for me on the doorstep. I went out, and she locked the door behind us, we left the patio table outside and headed quickly up the path—I didn't breathe a word about what I'd found.

We hurried up the path, our hasty departure recalling the way we'd left the house the night of the great fire at summer's end, leaving everything in place, not looking back, there was the same ill-considered haste about it, the same urgency about getting to the truck as soon as possible. When we reached the lot, I rolled the tarp off her father's old truck, hoisted the suitcase into its bed, and tried to wedge it tight, tie it down with bungees, while Marie put the truck into reverse. I ran alongside it for a few yards, and giving up on the bungees, leaving the suitcase tied down with a single secured hook around its handle, I joined Marie in the old truck as she was already accelerating down the road.

When we passed Maurizio's house at the end of the road, I leaned out to see if Giuseppe had stopped by his mother's after dropping us off. The house looked no different from before, the shutters were still closed and the patio empty, but there was no sign of Giuseppe's pickup nearby. Marie didn't even spare the house a glance, she headed down the road toward Portoferraio. She drove with an inscrutable expression, her anger cold, her rage suppressed, exacerbated. Something like this would never have happened while Maurizio was around, she said, he'd never have let anyone sleep in the house while we were gone—not even enter the house, no one would ever have so much as set foot inside while we were gone except for Maurizio himself, or a handyman, whom he would've been with and watched over and walked out, a mason or a plumber over for some minor routine maintenance or repairs. Now Maurizio's been dead a week and the house is already a hideout, a safe house for *latitanti!* (she said the word in Italian, *latitanti*, making it ring as she relished her disgust), and for her, the man to blame had a name, no doubt about it: Giuseppe.

Upon reaching Portoferraio, Marie crossed town, seeming
to know exactly where she was going. She headed straight
for the old port, resolute, determined, slowed beneath the
arcades of the *Porta a Mare*, and immediately parked in the
lot in the middle of the square. We got out of the truck.
Marie hadn't hesitated for a moment, as if she'd always
known where we were going ever since leaving Rivercina
(though doubtless she'd had no idea, wholly preoccupied
as she'd been with leaving the place as soon as possible). It
had stopped raining a few minutes ago, the ground was still
wet in the parking lot. Hesitating, suitcase at her feet, Marie
looked at the houses around her, the great pink and ochre
buildings with green shutters and tiled roofs. In the square,
not far from the cathedral, I recognized the façade of the
Ape Elbana Inn, where I'd stayed the year before when I'd
come to join Marie on Elba for her father's funeral. Faced
with Marie's indecision, it was I who took things in hand. I
picked up her suitcase and set off purposefully for the hotel.
I climbed the little flight of steps, went inside, and asked
the lady who, after a moment, turned up at the front desk
(perhaps the very same who'd welcomed me a year ago) if
she had a room available. Yes, practically all the rooms in
the hotel were available.

The lady escorted us to the second floor and opened the door to a room at the top of the stairs, a very spacious, high-ceilinged room with a double bed. The furniture was past its prime, Formica nightstands, a greenish chiffon bedspread, there were hardly any rugs on the old flecked linoleum flooring. Another bed, a folding bed, stood against one wall by a round table ringed with chairs, atop which sat a diminutive television. As a whole, it was fairly uncoordinated and incoherent, but the space was wonderful and three large windows, Persian blinds shut over their upper halves, overlooked the square. No sooner had the lady entered than she crossed to the radiators and cranked the knobs all the way, going from one radiator to the next, turning all three of them up to the max. *Aspettate un attimo*, she said, and explained we'd have to wait a few minutes for the heat to kick in. It was indeed quite cold in the room, maybe even colder than outside. She set the keys down on the table and left. We made a tour of the room, keeping our coats on. Marie cracked open the door to the commode, glanced inside, and shut it again. I turned on the television—hard to say if it was working or not—let the button pop back up under my finger, turning it off. We went to the window, opened the blinds, and gazed out over the square. We had nothing special to do, and we didn't linger long in the room.

We left the hotel. Even now, in the streets of Portoferraio, the smell of chocolate still prevailed. The air of the town was intimately imbued with it. That morning at daybreak, it must have been a burning smell that made itself known in the gray dawn, while smoke from the fire inland, borne on the wind, must have wandered the alleys at length before gradually dispersing. But now the smell had completely changed in nature, and when I went out in the street, I felt like I was getting a big whiff of hot chocolate. It was as if, over time, the initially stifling burning smell had shed whatever was sickening about it—the deleterious and toxic emanations, the hints of burnt rubber—uncorking instead, like a wine or perfume, to reveal more subtle charms—a note of pepper, a tang of citrus or orangettes—which, not having had enough time to express themselves earlier, had remained in hibernation behind the powerful dominant burning smell. Smell that? It smells like chocolate, Marie said, smiling, and began sniffing at the air, her nose upturned, openly breathing it in, hands in her coat pockets, as we walked to the truck.

We carried the exquisite chocolate aroma with us, so that, as we crossed town, it seemed to float everywhere in the atmosphere, above the old port all the way to the ramparts of the citadel, beneath the grayish skies of Portoferraio, impalpable, rich, milky, and vanilla-sweet, a bewitching chocolate aroma. It wasn't raining anymore, but the sky still looked threatening, thick black clouds were gathering in the distance, and large dark puddles stretched across the wet roads. At the traffic circle by the cement works, instead of taking the road to Rivercina as usual, Marie made a right turn toward the cemetery, and we traveled the deserted little streets of an inland part of town unfamiliar to us. Soon we could see the municipal stadium, the empty soccer field behind the fence, with vacant goals and a little covered seating area. The cemetery was right across the street. Marie parked the truck, and we headed for the cemetery on foot. I thought I saw Giuseppe's pickup parked on the shoulder, and the uneasy feeling that immediately came over me at the sight of that big black truck made me realize that running into Giuseppe at the funeral would be unpleasant.

A certain liveliness prevailed around the cemetery, cars were pulling up, people passing through the tall chain-link gates in small groups. On this, the eve of All Saints' Day, a few temporary florists' stands had popped up on the sidewalk, modest, rough-and-ready setups, trestle tables that wet umbrellas sheltered from the rain. A white van was parked on the sidewalk, and through its open doors a supply of flowers could be made out in back. Potted plants and several varieties of blooms were lined up on the stands. Marie stopped and bought a bouquet for Maurizio. She didn't want chrysanthemums and, moving along the displays, hesitant, indecisive, here and there picking up a bouquet to sniff or putting another back, she finally opted for a bouquet of lilies, six white lilies still largely closed, only one among them had blossomed.

We went through the cemetery gates, wordlessly following the other people headed, like us, to Maurizio's funeral, or who were simply there to honor their dead. Scattered groups of two or three people apiece, bouquets in hand, made their way along, chattering, sometimes pausing for a moment, and we moved on in silence down a cypress-lined lane. We emerged into a vast enclosed courtyard, not unlike the inner courtyard of a convent, whose walls were completely covered in funerary niches. Several people were already there, perched on ladders or little stepstools, arranging flowers in earthenware vases built into the marble plaques of the funerary niches. A family had even managed to drive their hatchback up, parking it in the middle of a gravel path, and they were busy around the open trunk, the father with the help of two daughters lifting out bags of potting soil. They had planted the nonagenarian uncle on a folding canvas chair at the foot of a pillar and the progenitor remained there, unmoving, a woolen *odio la Juve* beanie on his head, staring fixedly at the rows of funerary niches facing him. On our way out of the courtyard, we saw a crowd beside a grave in the distance, and Marie quickened her pace to join the group—but it wasn't Maurizio's funeral.

Imperceptibly, Marie was getting worried, she kept looking around her, disoriented, afraid she'd gotten the time wrong, setting out first this way and then that, retracing her steps. She headed tentatively down a smaller path, which we followed till it dead-ended in a willow grove in the shadow of the outer wall. There the mournful sight of a raw concrete mausoleum loomed before us, its niches entirely empty, a dull grayish wall with about sixty empty alcoves awaiting urns. Marie pulled her cell phone from her coat pocket and said she was going to call Francesco, Maurizio's older son, to find out where they were. She tried calling, but couldn't get a signal, I watched as she walked among the graves, phone pressed to her ear, going from one path to the next within the same tiny perimeter, before realizing the cemetery's outer wall might be blocking the signal, as if the dead, better able to preserve their serenity than the living, were absorbing the cell phone waves and immediately swallowing them up underground. To get around this obstacle, Marie started walking along the outer wall, looking for an opening that might let the waves through. She finally found a little side gate that gave out on an empty street and, standing right beside the opening, pressed up against the bars, she dialed Francesco's number, but got his voicemail. She left a message and hung up. She hesitated for a moment, looked at me. Giuseppe? I nodded, and she dialed Giuseppe's number. I saw her anxious face as she waited, eyes tense, gaze fixed on something in the distance. Giuseppe didn't answer either, and Marie seemed almost relieved. She left no message and put the phone away as we began walking again, hurrying down the pathways, not knowing where to go anymore.

We had no idea where Maurizio's funeral was, and ahead of me in the cemetery, Marie pressed on, lost, amidst the monotony of the pathways, bouquet in hand, uncertain, looking all around her. To either side of us, on the neat lawns, graves stretched as far as the eye could see. What struck my eye was that all these graves were in flower for the day of the dead, not a single one had been forgotten, not even the most remote, the merest mound or tumulus topped by a cross. It was flowers everywhere, in pots, vases, window boxes, it was baskets of daisies, marguerites, spindle trees, and veronica, it was fresh flowers gathered from gardens that day or the night before, alive, beaming, luminous, it was thousands of flowers in every color whose bright spots of vivid hues stood out in the gray day—the yellow of gladioli, the orange of nasturtiums, the blue-red, almost mauve, of violets—it was wreaths and bouquets, pink cyclamen in pots, irises, dahlias, and more, and always, forever, everywhere, chrysanthemums, chrysanthemums of all sorts blooming in the damp mist that lay over the cemetery's pathways. Sometimes it was also, more sadly, artificial flowers, ceramic flowers, pale and wasting away, their colors soft and fading, deep purple or faded pink, porcelain flowers, forgotten flowers, grieving flowers that went well with the speckled gray of old graves, over which they seemed to be pining away.

Marie pointed into the distance and said it had to be that way, then took a narrow path down a gentle slope where the graves, more austere, less spaced out, huddled up against one another. We could see nothing now, the horizon was black, blocked out in every direction by a dark line of sepulchers. On every side rose the imposing masses of family vaults, which looked like chapels, often protected by a fence and topped with a cross. Marie was going slower, carefully guiding me through the maze of funerary monuments, as if she knew the way and any moment now we were about to emerge right onto the scene of Maurizio's funeral. There was something almost urban about this narrow, steep-sided part of the cemetery, with its aisles and intersections, we were in a veritable necropolis, a hamlet of the dead, absolutely deserted, derelict, silent, its ever-darker alleys fading into the distant gloom. Most of the mausoleums were surrounded by fences and little yards, and seemed abandoned, but sometimes a lighted chamber could be made out through a window, with vases full of flowers on the floor, sometimes a saucer, fruits and cakes. I don't know if the presence of these offerings were in keeping with ancestral Mediterranean customs for an ancient feast of the dead that urged families to leave milk and chestnuts meant for the deceased, but it wasn't uncommon to find, on the floors of these funerary chambers visible through vault windows, among floral offerings, surrounded by candles whose flames shivered in the gloom, a bottle of mineral water and a few abandoned cookies.

I gazed at the tortured skies above. Great black rain clouds were moving in and covering the cemetery. The light was crepuscular, almost blue in places. It wasn't the first time today I'd gotten the feeling it was nighttime in the middle of the day in Portoferraio, I'd felt as much stepping off the boat that morning when thick black smoke from the fire was darkening the quays and making it seem like day hadn't yet broken in Portoferraio. Just then, it began to rain—and right from the first moment it started raining, right from the very second, that smell came back to mind, that smell we'd forgotten for a moment, which the rain had just revived, freeing its fragrance into the air, releasing its aromas, that chocolate smell suddenly making itself felt all around us among the marble tombs. There was no escaping that piercing smell, we hastened our step among the funerary monuments, but we were moving in the very smell itself, no longer pleasant or picturesque at all, but now of a radically changed nature, grown nauseating, mingling with the abstract odor of death that held sway in the cemetery, an odor of decomposition, putrefaction, the organic odor of dead bodies, the smooth, sickly sweet, repulsive smell of chocolate that would follow us all afternoon, which we couldn't get rid of, and which, now blending with the falling rain, dissolving in it, stuck to our skin and hair, soaked our clothes, penetrated our eyes, and streaked down our cheeks. We rubbed our cheeks with our fingers to get away from it, still pressing on between two rows of vaults that seemed to hem us in, that chocolate smell which seemed to pour from the sky like sticky pine resin and cover Marie's coat, slowly glazing it, enrobing it, dusting it with a fine chocolaty veneer.

The smell seemed to be materializing right before our eyes now, we saw it take shape with the rain, which seeped slowly from the sky, which oozed, dirty, dark, brownish, a sticky drizzle, ferruginously black, that seemed equal parts burnt chocolate from the Monte Capanne factory and rust from the disused open-pit iron mines around Rio Marina. But that poisoned chocolate air was the very air we had to breathe, the one and only air we could breathe in that cemetery, that bitter air laden with cocoa vapors mixed with the smells of iron ore, magnetite, and pyrite, seasoned by whiffs of cinnabar, mercury, and sulfur. Everything around us—the air, the soil, the darkness itself—seemed thinned, melted, liquefied, so that it seemed to coat us, viscidly, in a continuous downpour of fine, clingy, chocolaty rain. The mausoleum walls were streaming with rain, and we could see chocolate mist rising from the wet headstones, while the organic juices of the deceased seemed to seep from the marble of the sodden sepulchers. Marie, getting ever further ahead of me, felt faint, one hand on her mouth, eyes wild, her sense of smell assailed, no longer able to bear the odor of chocolate, which made her want to vomit. She'd turned around, she was retracing her steps, she was fleeing, giving up on the idea of finding Maurizio's funeral, not even looking for it anymore, it didn't even matter to her now, all she wanted was to get out of here, leave the cemetery, find some fresh air again, be rid of that nagging odor that was making her nauseous. And then, lost, backtracking, with no idea where the exit was, Marie felt sick, Marie almost fainted.

She tottered on her feet, looking for a wall to lean on, somewhere to sit, a bench, a chair, but finding only graves as far
as she could see, she staggered a few more feet and finally
collapsed on a marble tombstone. She was very pale, and as
I ran up to help her, she was overcome by another brief fit
of trembling, just like this morning, which left her sapped,
exhausted, unable to react, to get up, to take another step.
She kept trembling there, on the spot, ever more slowly,
head sagging. I leaned over and, gently, to soothe her, asked
her what was going on. What's the matter, Marie? I whispered, what's wrong? What's wrong? she said, looking up at
me, can't you tell? I'm pregnant.

On the way back from the cemetery, just as we were getting
in the truck, I asked Marie if she wanted me to drive, but
she said no, she felt up to it (she was pregnant, not sick,
she said), and got behind the wheel, setting the bouquet of
shriveled, rain-soaked lilies on the dash. We were quiet for
a moment in the cab. My thoughts were racing, so many
things that had seemed strange to me lately were suddenly
clear, while so many others stubbornly persisted in remaining obscure. And then, turning toward her, I said with sudden intuition, "So that was it, then, the thing you wanted
to tell me that night at the café in Saint-Sulpice?" I said it
without thinking, as if it were undeniable, something I'd

always known but hadn't managed to put into words, and she gave a slow, painful nod.

Marie had started the truck, and we drove away from the cemetery past Portoferraio's municipal stadium. I thought we were going back to the hotel but, when we reached the traffic circle by the cement works, Marie surprised me by heading toward Rivercina. She explained that she wanted to give Antonina, Maurizio's wife, a hug, and since she didn't know where the funeral was, suggested we go and wait for the family at Maurizio's house in Rivercina, where his loved ones would no doubt gather after the ceremony.

A few miles before reaching Rivercina, as we were passing by a little chapel, we saw an unusual number of cars parked every which way by the side of the road, some at an angle and some on the side of the embankment, thirty-odd cars filling every last available space on the shoulder. It was there, a bit further up, in a family vault hidden in the foliage, that Maurizio's funeral must have taken place. Marie had slowed and was now crawling along, watching the undergrowth to try and spot the unseen vault from the road. It looked like the ceremony had just ended, for people were appearing from every direction in little groups of two or three, seeming to emerge from the trees as if by spontaneous generation, flowing down the hill toward the road with the slow inexorability of trickling water. The crowd reached the cars, the oldest and most infirm along a marked trail, with close family grouped around Maurizio's wife, Antonina, whom her eldest son escorted with a hand on her arm.

Marie got out of the car as soon as she saw Antonina. She grabbed the bouquet on the dash, opened the door, and raced out to meet her. She ran across the road and burst into tears in Antonina's arms, giving free rein to all the emotion that had been building up for the last few hours, the last few days, ever since she'd learned of Maurizio's death, all that suppressed, repressed, bottled-up emotion she'd more or less managed to control till now. There had always been something incomparable about Marie's emotions, a quality which had less to do with the actual circumstances causing them than the *oceanic affinity* I'd perceived in her, which honed her sensitivity, exacerbated it, made her feelings quiver with uncommon intensity. The old woman seemed as moved as Marie, I'd noticed the look in her eye, that brief flash of surprise, rapture, and pain when she saw Marie running toward her. For in that embrace, Marie was also standing in for her father, she was symbolically his representative, such that, vicariously, Marie was giving Antonina the hug her father might have given the old woman upon learning of Maurizio's death. But it was even more, for Antonina, that old woman dressed in a white lace shirt and a belted black vest, that fragile little lady, buttressed by her eldest son, was the only person who'd known Marie as a child. I watched Marie from a distance, and felt that rather than Marie crying, distraught, in Antonina's arms, it was instead the little girl she'd been thirty years ago. Still holding on tightly to Antonina and talking to her at the same time, Marie gave her the bouquet of flowers, turned to greet everyone else, burst into laughter pointing at the poor frazzled bouquet she'd just given Antonina, for with Marie laughter and tears were never far apart, and she stepped aside to solemnly embrace Francesco, Maurizio's oldest son, in a black suit and white shirt, whom I too, when I joined them, would take in my arms.

Marie realized then that Giuseppe, Maurizio's other son, had kept his distance from our group and was watching us off to one side with his weary, bored air. He was about to leave again, but Marie didn't give him a chance to, she went straight over and demanded an explanation. At first, Giuseppe recoiled from the assault, seeming to dodge the question, throwing one arm up in a show of anger, impotence, or denial. He tried to keep Marie at bay, fending her off with an irate hand. He was trying to get to his pickup,

but he couldn't manage to shake her. Marie chased him
to the edge of the road, taking him aside, whispering ever
more loudly, suddenly breaking into a screeching hiss at
the side of the road, so that several people looked their way
to see what was happening. Marie, a bulldog, kept after
him, not letting him off the hook, and when he'd reached
his big pickup parked sloppily sideways on the hill, since
Giuseppe was about to get away, Marie screamed "*Che ver-
gogna!*" Everyone turned to stare at them. Furious, Giuseppe
got in his pickup and put it in gear, hurtling down the hill
in reverse without looking where he was going and almost
running over Marie—who'd stayed right where she was, not
budging an inch—only missing her immovable body in the
middle of the road at the last minute by jerking the wheel,
before taking off at top speed, tires squealing behind him,
like the cretin he was. Then Marie, rigid in the middle of the
road, her face unreadable, her upper lip quivering slightly,
watched him drive away and just now, belatedly, warding
off the danger she'd just dodged, she made the unexpected
gesture of slowly folding one hand, then the other, before
herself to protect her belly.

We had gotten back in the truck, and Marie remained sitting
for a moment, motionless at the wheel, still a bit shocked
by the incident. We'd double-parked in the middle of the

road, and the departing cars passed us or turned awkwardly around us, the drivers staring at us for a moment through the windshield, refraining from honking their horns—obsequies obliging, of course. Lost in her thoughts, Marie was utterly indifferent to the fact that she was blocking traffic, she was slowly pulling herself back together. Finally she started the truck again, made a U-turn a bit further up, and we headed back toward Portoferraio. I kept my eyes on the road, and I was thinking that we had come to Elba for Maurizio's funeral, that we had come all the way from Paris for his last rites, and that had been it just now, Maurizio's funeral, that was it, a few fleeting minutes by the side of the road, dashing from the truck with the motor still running, a little gushing, and a brief altercation with Giuseppe on the shoulder. And already it was over, done with, now we were on our way back to the hotel. I stared at the road, a bit woozy on the winding roads of Elba, and I mused about this failure, which reminded me of another, on the same order, one day when I'd gone to pay a visit to my uncle at the cemetery. I'd headed for his grave but, unable to find it, had gotten lost among the many paths and left the cemetery without ever seeing it. Later, as another experience of the same sort was happening to me again, I reflected on the singular act of not finding someone you'd gone to see in a cemetery, and realized that this misadventure revealed, at its heart, the true nature of any visit to a cemetery, which was that, when you go to see people in a cemetery, it's natural not to see them, entirely natural not to find them, for they cannot be found, ever, instead you are confronted with their absence, their irremediable absence. And then I thought that, if Marie hadn't found Maurizio's grave this afternoon, if she'd gotten the cemetery wrong when we'd come all the way from Paris for the funeral, it was because she hadn't *wanted* to find the right cemetery, and if she hadn't *wanted* to find it, it was because it wasn't death she wanted to talk to me about during our stay in Elba—but life.

Marie drove another few miles without saying anything, lost as ever in her thoughts, before pulling over on a small esplanade overlooking the sea. She cut the engine. She kept staring straight ahead pensively, her face solemn, unfathomable. Then she took my arm gently, and told me she was sorry she'd announced the news of her pregnancy so abruptly earlier. That wasn't how she'd imagined it happening. She'd planned instead to tell me after Maurizio's funeral, once that was all over and done with, so as not to mix everything up. Like now, you mean? She mulled it over. Yes, like now (so, uh, hey, I'm pregnant, she told me).

Once back at the hotel, we had the unpleasant surprise of

finding out the radiators in the room still weren't working, they were still as cold as they'd been when we got in, the white cast-iron under my hand was positively icy. I went down to the front desk and the lady, who seemed as surprised as she was sorry about the inconvenience, assured me she'd see to it right way, and do everything she could to fix the problem as soon as possible. I rejoined Marie in the room. She hadn't yet taken off her coat, and was gazing thoughtfully past the double doors of the wardrobe she'd opened at the handful of hangers dangling in the emptiness. It was only a little past four, and even if we'd decided to dine early, we couldn't reasonably show up at a restaurant in the old port before seven, seven-thirty. Almost three hours lay between us and dinner, three empty hours, vacant, stretching before us like a vast and dizzying void.

I'd lain down on the bed in my coat, hands in my pockets (a leopard can't change its spots), and was staring at the ceiling, as completely at loose ends as I'd been in Tokyo shortly after our separation. I stared at the ceiling, not directly, but a bit sidelong, and that particular way of staring at the ceiling, with an imperceptible slant to my gaze (associative thinking hangs by a thread sometimes), reminded me then not of the ceiling of the hotel room in Tokyo where I'd wound up, but of the state of mind I'd found myself in then,

during those endless hours when I'd stay flat on my back
not doing a thing in that Tokyo hotel room, pondering the
bitter truth that asserted itself in me more acutely with each
passing day, that days are always unspeakably long and life
tragically short.

Marie had opened the window and pushed open a shutter,
and she was now gazing at the pink and ochre façades of
the square. Though it wasn't dark yet, the streetlights were
already on. Before us we could see the orange glow of lanterns hung from houses, their halos beginning to tinge the
still daylit air of the square. Marie had lit a cigarette, and was
smoking silently by the window. I saw her in her coat from
behind, her wrist bent slightly back, her delicate hand holding a cigarette between its fingers. It was the same image,
exactly the same—her posture, the steadiness of her profile,
smoke slowly rising from the motionless cigarette—as that
of Marie at the café on Place Saint-Sulpice two days ago,
when I'd watched her in the night through the windows.
And even if, at that moment in Saint-Sulpice, I couldn't yet
have guessed that Marie was pregnant, in truth I'd known
it already, it was there, in Saint-Sulpice, that I'd known for
the first time she was pregnant. In some subliminal way, I'd
known from that image, as if the invisible had entered my
field of vision, and eternity into time. I realized then that

my mind had always turned everything important in my life into images, and that these scenes which might have seemed innocuous at first, which remained prosaic, contingent, or fortuitous, so deeply buried were they in real life where they'd taken place, these scenes gradually became, as my mind took them up again, reworked them, steeped in them, and chewed them over, new material which I reshaped to my liking, the better to reveal and bring to light a completely new image, as much the invention of memory as emotion, reminiscence as sensibility. And it was this new vision, transformed and enriched, that fixed itself forever in my memory to form the matrix of my recollections to come. Lying on the bed in that hotel room in Portoferraio, I knew with certainty that when I later remembered the moment when Marie had told me she was pregnant—and remember it I would, all my life, for it was one of those moments you don't forget—those two scenes would become superimposed in my mind, equally pertinent, equally legitimate, the virtual scene in Paris, in that café on Place Saint-Sulpice, where I'd guessed she was pregnant without managing to put an exact word to her condition (the negative of the scene, in a way, already exposed in my mind but not yet developed), and the actual scene, a few hours ago on Elba, when Marie had really told me she was pregnant.

And I thought then that these two scenes actually resembled Annunciations, the first in Saint-Sulpice, a contemporary Annunciation, a twenty-first-century image with that digital look, the night and the strong presence of rain, traces of scattered droplets on the windows, a Nan Goldin photo with Marie's face glimpsed between the streaks of headlights of a No. 87 bus, cheekbones damp and hair disheveled, recalling that famous Hopper painting, a night scene in a diner, the hieratic figures each imprisoned in their own solitude, a soda jerk in profile behind the counter, and Marie's red dress (maybe just renaming Hopper's painting *Annunciation* instead of *Nighthawks* would be all it took to completely transfigure the vision?). The scene in Portoferraio, however, the actual scene the two of us had lived today, seemed less part of the twenty-first century that had given rise to it than part of a more ancient pictorial tradition, that of the Italian Renaissance Annunciations. First the setting, similar to that of a Florentine painting, the cemetery's Tuscan landscape—a few cypresses, the sky, the veined marble where Marie had sat down—the arrangement of the figures, Marie to the right and me standing, leaning over her (but in this composition I was there only to draw attention to her, Marie played all the roles: at once the angel Gabriel and Mary, her namesake). But it was above all the iconographic details that struck me in their astonishing propinquity: Marie's outfit, her lightweight cream woolen coat, which had the immaculate whiteness of depictions of purity, not to mention her bouquet, the white lilies she was holding, which are found purposefully depicted in many Renaissance paintings. And yet, despite these multiple similarities, it seemed something was out of place in this comparison, and what was out of place, in my opinion, was Mary's expression when she got the news, Mary who, in every version of an Annunciation from the Renaissance, always had a particularly gentle, majestic, and reverential face attesting to self-effacement, acceptance, even submission. And yet the way Marie had told me she was pregnant this afternoon, the way she'd flung it right in my face in the Portoferraio cemetery, with vehemence in her eyes, had something violent and alarming about it. It wasn't a confession, it was a reproach. And as I went on pondering, I remembered Botticelli's *Annunciation* in the Uffizi, whose Virgin bears an astonishing psychological resemblance to Marie's state of mind that afternoon in the Portoferraio cemetery, that Botticelli Virgin who is, to the best of my knowledge, the sole example in the history of Italian Annunciations of this reticent posture on the Virgin's part, a deep-seated, fundamental reticence, which seems in a single gesture to bear witness to both acceptance and refusal of her condition, her sinuous figure and her raised hand—as if Botticelli had painted not an Annunciation but a *Noli me tangere!*

Marie had smoked half her cigarette at the window. She took another drag, her gaze lost in the distance over the square. Only then, belatedly, was I surprised she was still smoking despite being pregnant. You're still smoking? I said. She turned to me and softly explained that she hardly smoked at all anymore, well, still one or two cigarettes a day—this was the first today, she said, staring carefully at her cigarette—and added that she was planning to quit, she'd probably quit next week as soon as we got back to Paris. She didn't even finish her cigarette, just slowly, pensively drilled it into the windowsill to put it out. When Marie had mentioned our going back to Paris, I'd noticed the "we," and I had the feeling our relationship was about to take a new turn. For just as a crack sometimes appears a couple's relationship, which with time can only widen and worsen until it ends up a definitive rift, I felt that for us it was rather in the very principle of our breakup that a fissure was appearing, a fissure that, with what we'd just been through and the fact that Marie was pregnant, could only grow, until if it grew any wider, the very idea of our separation would be threatened (and we would wind up, sooner or later, living together again).

I wondered why Marie hadn't told me she was pregnant earlier. When I asked her, she simply said she'd wanted to wait until she was sure. We made small talk for another ten minutes or so in the room, with her still standing at the window in her coat, and me lying on the bed. Besides, she said, she hadn't suspected a thing all September, it was only in mid-October, noticing her period was late, that she'd been intrigued, but she hadn't really believed it yet, since she hadn't had sex that summer—except with me, of course, one little time toward the end (but those were such special circumstances that it didn't count for her, she explained, smiling). When Marie had informed me she was pregnant, I myself had been so surprised that for a moment I'd doubted I was the father, since we had indeed not had sex for several months, save for that brief embrace the night of the great fire at summer's end when, in the wee small hours, we'd furtively united in the darkness of the room, exhausted and bruised, an embrace more of consolation and affection than actual sexual intercourse in due and proper form (but apparently that had counted too, we must've been misinformed). Then, about two weeks ago, Marie had started having serious suspicions, and made an appointment with her gynecologist. She'd only gotten tested at the beginning of the week, and it was that same day, Monday afternoon, she'd found out both about her pregnancy and Maurizio's death, via a call from Francesco a bit later in the evening. But when Marie had phoned me to meet up in Saint-Sulpice, it was with every intention of telling me she was pregnant. One last thing remained a mystery to me: why had she dropped me since the end of summer, why—whether pregnant or not—hadn't I heard a word from her for two months after getting back from Elba? When I asked her why, she remained evasive, and for a moment I thought she didn't want to answer the question, that maybe she had something to hide. Then she turned and stared at me thoughtfully. What, like you called me?

We'd been back at the hotel for about ten minutes when there was a knock at the door, and without waiting for an answer, the hotel lady came in with her husband and a fellow in blue overalls carrying a toolbox, a repairman if there ever was one. All three of them came into the room and went straight over to the radiators. I got up quickly (as if it were somehow unseemly to be lying on one's bed in a hotel room) and Marie, hands in her coat pockets, moved away instinctively from the window, a kind of silent choreography played out in the room, each of us stepping back to let the others by or, quite the opposite, spreading out to take up all the available space. Precise, methodical, sparing of gesture, the repairman set his toolbox on the table and immediately went to shut the window, looking at us reproachfully (just shutting the window might have been a good start if we were cold, then maybe we'd have had less reason to complain downstairs). After whacking the cast-iron a few times with a hammer, and observing that it sounded hollow (with a touch of smugness, as in: I knew it), he told the lady that the radiators would have to be bled, and as Marie and I were obviously in their way, not knowing what to do with ourselves during the repairs, finding ourselves more or less in the hallway, we ended up stepping out of the hotel.

It was now completely dark outside, streetlights were on all around the square, casting an orangish glow here and there on the damp asphalt. We turned for a moment to look back at the façade of the hotel we were leaving behind, its lighted sign had just gone on. Marie headed for the parking lot and went straight to her father's truck. She didn't hesitate for a second. Rather than wandering around the edges of the old port for an hour, waiting for the repairman to finish up, she'd decided to take her father's truck back to Rivercina to save some time so we could take the first boat out of Elba the next morning, as early as possible (we'd hop a taxi back from Rivercina). She started the engine, and we left town. Soon after the traffic circle by the cement works, there were no more lights along the road. After a few miles through the countryside, we zipped past the Monte Capanne chocolate factory's depots sunk in gloom. There were no more police roadblocks up at the factory, nothing to slow down traffic, as we passed by all I could make out in the night were silhouettes of dark buildings that still emanated a vague, almost imperceptible smell of burning.

As we neared the turn leading to Rivercina, Marie, seeing a light on in Maurizio's house, suddenly slowed, kept crawling along for a few yards, then stopped, pulled over on the shoulder, and cut the lights, first the headlights, then the sidelights. All the shutters on Maurizio's house were still closed, but light could be seen coming through the slits in the blinds, and two cars were parked on the concrete terrace in front of the house, Giuseppe's big black pickup and a carabinieri car. We stayed quietly in the truck for a moment, watching the house closely through the windshield. There wasn't a single sound. Marie had just pulled over on the side of the road, I don't know what made her wait, but after a minute, four or five people came out of the house, uniformed carabinieri with Giuseppe among them, hanging back a bit, head low, surrounded by policemen. Giuseppe, we knew, had dubious relations with the police, a stoolpigeon maybe, or a collaborator, I don't know, we'd seen him talking this morning with a plainclothes detective, but it seemed like he had no arrangement with these policemen, everyone was silent, their faces somber, what we were watching was more like someone being taken away for questioning. Still, some doubt remained, some ambiguity, for Giuseppe wasn't in handcuffs, and at no moment did the carabinieri touch him, take him by the arm, or force him into the car, but he did get in the backseat, and two carabinieri got in, one on either side of him, while the other two got in front. The car full of carabinieri turned around in the cramped terrace in front of the house, came out the gate, and headed straight for us, headlights beaming, such that from the backseat Giuseppe must have glimpsed us for a moment in the headlights' glare. The carabinieri car passed us and drove off, and only then did I see Antonina on the doorstep, small, stiff, her face hard, unreadable, an expression of dignity and controlled pain, her figure in the pool of light from a bulb above the front door. She stayed like that for a moment, scanning the horizon, then went back in, and closed the door behind her.

Marie started the truck again, but didn't turn on the headlights, and headed down the road to Rivercina in the dark, going slow and parking in the shed. We got out of the car, the night was without a sound, we heard a little owl in the distance. We took the path down to the house to drop off the keys to the truck and call a taxi. As we reached the patio, we saw a massive, motionless shadow against the wall, which we struggled to identify until we realized it was the heavy wrought-iron table we'd left outside. We went up to the front door, Marie slid the key in the lock, pushed open the door, and stopped short: there was light coming from upstairs. I was just behind her, she hadn't moved, her hand on the knob, brought up short, frozen in place. Anyone home? I said, walking around her, looking toward the landing. I told Marie I'd go upstairs and check. I walked over to the stairs and started up. Anyone home? I said again, shouted, really, halfway up the stairs, and that was when I realized that if someone was there, that someone was hiding, it was some-one who didn't want to show himself, someone who didn't want to answer my questions—especially not if they were in French. So it was someone who wouldn't move from where they were, someone I'd have to find myself, someone I'd have to physically confront in Marie's room, and I would doubtless have been much less frightened to see someone above me now in the hallway than to have to confront that silent darkness, unmoving and deceptive, over which I had no control. I'd reached the top of the stairs. I made my way down the hall slowly, pausing before the door, and went into Marie's room. I didn't really go in, a quick glance was all it took to size up the situation, take stock of the various elements, the unmade bed, the wardrobe, the fatigues dis-carded by the chair. Nothing had moved since this morning,

the room was empty, there was no one around. I switched
off the light and retraced my steps. I went down the stairs,
feeling my way along in the dark while reassuring Marie,
telling her we were alone in the house, we must've just forgotten to turn out the light when leaving this morning.

Marie was waiting for me at the foot of the stairs, she hadn't
turned the light on or shut the front door. She hadn't moved.
She took my hand then, and led me into the silent house.
She guided me through the dark, through the living room,
where we made out the shapes of furniture in the shadows,
and steered me to the ground floor room where I'd slept last
summer. She pushed me inside, following after, and without
turning on the light, threw herself at me, kissing me, and I
realized then why she'd insisted on leading me to this room,
because it was here, in this room, that we'd made love last
summer, and the two scenes superimposed themselves in my
mind, I found myself in the present and the past all at once,
in the final days of August, when Marie had come to my
room in the wee small hours, and now, swaying in Marie's
arms in the total darkness of this hermetically sealed room,
whose window was blocked by a nailed-up shutter. The place
was the same, the people the same, our feelings the same,
only the season had changed, fall had taken the place of
summer, we were both wearing coats now, whereas Marie

had been naked under her tee shirt when she'd joined me under the sheets then. And so, still pressed together in the room, clinging to each other, tottering, tripping over the furniture, bumping into the barbecue, we stumbled to the bed, and let ourselves fall onto it. We kissed in the dark, with enthusiasm, distress, confidence, love, how fragile Marie felt in my arms, we held each other tightly, madly, as we had two months ago in this very bed, our bodies joining, our lives uniting, our souls reaching equilibrium, to soothe our tensions, release the worries that had been oppressing us for so long, dissolve them, make them disappear, I ran my hands over her face, Marie had taken my head between her hands and was kissing me with an intensity she'd never shown before, I felt her tongue in my mouth, her soft, impassioned, ardent, uninhibited tongue, cool at first then slightly salty, Marie who was crying in my arms, I couldn't see her face in the dark, it wasn't my eyes that told me she was crying, but my tongue, I tasted her tears in my mouth. Everything was damp, aqueous, fluid, her tears and our saliva mingling in the dark. Don't cry, I whispered, gently caressing her hair, and she shook her head no, she told me she wasn't crying, she was just so happy, and started crying even harder, she was still kissing me, sniffling slightly, and, lapping at her tears with my tongue, to mingle them with our kisses, still kissing me, barely opening her mouth, she said, murmured, in a breath, in our embrace, in the kisses themselves, with a kind of astonishment, "Then you love me?"

JEAN-PHILIPPE TOUSSAINT is the author of nine novels and the winner of numerous literary prizes, including the Prix Décembre for *The Truth about Marie*, which is available from Dalkey Archive Press. His writing has been compared to the works of Samuel Beckett, Jacques Tati, Jim Jarmusch, and even Charlie Chaplin.

A graduate of the Iowa Writers' Workshop, EDWARD GAUVIN was a 2007 fellow at the American Literary Translators Association conference and received a residency from the Banff International Literary Translation Centre. His translation of Jean-Philippe Toussaint's *Urgency and Patience* was published by Dalkey Archive Press in 2015.